Meet the team:

Alex – A quiet lad from Northumbria, Alex leads the team in survival skills. His dad is in the SAS and Alex is determined to follow in his footsteps, whatever it takes. He who dares . . .

Li – Expert in martial arts and free-climbing, Li can get to grips with most situations . . .

Paulo – The laid-back Argentinian is a mechanical genius, and with his medical skills ca[illegible] up injuries as well as motors . . .

Hex – An ace hacker, ra[illegible] palmtop, Hex is first [illegible] can bypass most security sy[illegible]

Amber – Her top navigati[illegible]ills mean the team are rarely lost. Rarely lost for words either, rich-girl Amber can show some serious attitude . . .

With plenty of hard work and training, together they are **Alpha Force** – an elite squad dedicated to combating injustice throughout the world.

In *Black Gold*, Alpha Force are in the Caribbean. They are there to improve their scuba diving skills, but a tanker disaster and an assassin's bullet soon mean they have a new mission to undertake . . .

www.**kidsatrandomhouse**.co.uk/alphaforce

Don't miss any of the missions in the Alpha Force series:

SURVIVAL
RAT-CATCHER
DESERT PURSUIT
HOSTAGE
RED CENTRE
HUNTED
BLOOD MONEY
FAULT LINE
BLACK GOLD
UNTOUCHABLE

Also available by Chris Ryan, published by Arrow, for adult readers:

STAND BY, STAND BY
ZERO OPTION
THE KREMLIN DEVICE
TENTH MAN DOWN
THE HIT LIST
THE WATCHMAN
LAND OF FIRE
GREED

Non-fiction:

THE ONE THAT GOT AWAY
(the story of his experiences in the SAS and in Iraq)

CHRIS RYAN'S SAS FITNESS BOOK
CHRIS RYAN'S ULTIMATE SURVIVAL GUIDE

HERE'S WHAT READERS THINK OF THE ALPHA FORCE SERIES:

'Instantly readable, and I found it hard to put down. A cool read!' *Chris*

'All the Alpha Force series are great. Keep writin', Chris, the world of books will be boring without you!' *reader from Leeds*

'A really gripping read that is bound to keep your fingernails short' *Andrew, from New Zealand*

'This book had me hooked from the start: it was really cool . . . it was so amazing I went and bought the next one in the series!' *Lisa, from Wiltshire*

'To describe the book in one word – only one word suits the job, GREAT!' *reader from Cornwall*

'From the first page you are drawn into the story and you can't put it down. I was excited by every word. This book is amazing! Chris Ryan builds suspense better than J. K. Rowling! This gripping novel keeps you reading for hours and is ideal for 11–16-year-old boys and girls alike' *'Bookworm' Lizzi*

'I enjoyed this book because the characters were fun and the plot was interesting. The reader also finds out things that the characters do not know, so they act unpredictably creating unexpected twists and turns. I would recommend this book to teens because this is an action book where the heroes are teens themselves. It also contains the added bonus of Chris Ryan's top SAS tactics' *Thomas, from Middlesex*

'I bought this book for my brother and ended up reading it myself!' *Clare, from Plymouth*

'It keeps you wondering what will happen and has twists and turns all the way through'
Luke, from Lincolnshire

'I love these books and think they're really great. It's really great how Chris Ryan can write about such adult matters yet still make them young adults' books; they're a real inspiration! Rating: 10/10'
Kelly, from Edinburgh

BLACK GOLD

RED
FOX

ALPHA FORCE : BLACK GOLD
A RED FOX BOOK 9780099482321

First published in Great Britain by Red Fox,
an imprint of Random House Children's Publishers UK

This edition published 2005

10

Typeset in Sabon by Palimpsest Book Production Limited,
Polmont, Stirlingshire

The Random House Group Limited makes every effort to ensure that the papers used in our books are made from trees that have been legally sourced from well-managed and credibly certified forests. Our paper procurement policy can be found on www.randomhouse.co.uk/paper.htm.

Typeset in Sabon by Palimpsest Book Production Limited,
Polmont, Stirlingshire

Red Fox Books are published by Random House Children's Publishers UK,
61–63 Uxbridge Road, London W5 5SA,
A Random House Group Company

Addresses for companies within The Random House Group Limited can be found at: www.randomhouse.co.uk/offices.htm

THE RANDOM HOUSE GROUP Limited Reg. No. 954009
www.**randomhousechildrens**.co.uk

A CIP catalogue record for this book is available from the British Library.

The Random House Group Limited supports The Forest Stewardship Council (FSC®), the leading international forest certification organisation. Our books carrying the FSC label are printed on FSC® certified paper. FSC is the only forest certification scheme endorsed by the leading environmental organisations, including Greenpeace. Our paper procurement policy can be found at www.randomhouse.co.uk/environment

Printed and bound in Great Britain by Clays Ltd, St Ives PLC

ALPHA FORCE

The field of operation...

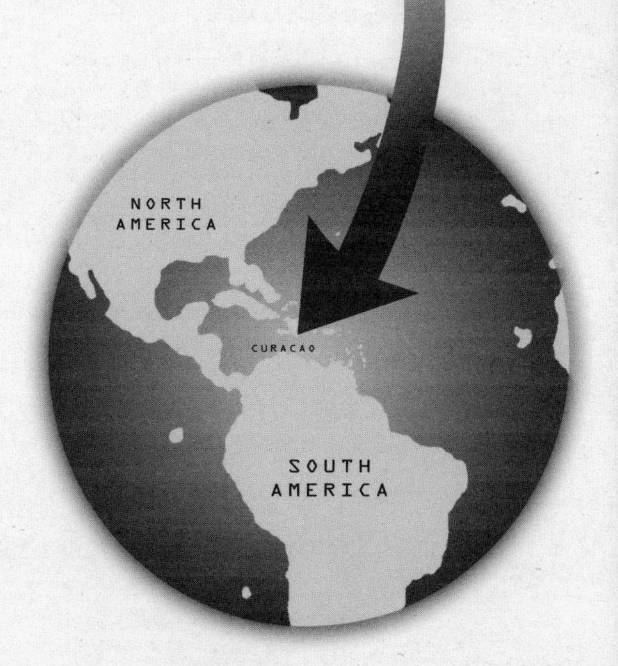

Prologue

Collision Course

The oil tanker ploughed a furrow through the Caribbean Sea. Its deck was the length of three football pitches, the living quarters rising out of the stern like a four-storey building, topped by a cluster of radio transmitters, whirling radar masts – and a flag bearing the red insignia of ArBonCo Oil.

Inside, at the very top of the tower, Tomas Amurao pushed open the door to the bridge and manoeuvred his mop and bucket inside. As he did so, he heard shouting. Two men – the captain and the second-in-command – were standing at the control station. The second-in-command was pointing to the radar screen, which showed a glowing dot touching the crosshairs of the screen. There was something out there, right in their path.

Out of the window Amurao could see the sea, a long way down, and a gleaming white passenger cruiser gliding past. It was a big ship with four decks, one with a glittering turquoise square of swimming pool, but the tanker towered over it like a skyscraper.

Amurao was Filipino and didn't understand the language the Dutch crewmen were speaking – but he couldn't mistake the meaning. They'd nearly hit the cruiser. How? He knew that there were numerous automatic systems to stop them colliding with other objects in the water.

He began to mop the floor by the door. The shouting stopped, and it was then that he realized what was so odd.

It was far too quiet.

Usually the bridge was noisy, the ship's control systems constantly bleeping and beeping, like birdsong in a jungle. But today they were silent. The only sound was the faint throb of the massive engines, deep below the water line.

What was going on? Amurao had spent two years as a deckhand on oil tankers and he'd never known one travel with the automatics off. Perhaps there had been a malfunction?

He took his bucket to the control area and mopped around the big metal lever that rose from the floor like a giant gearshift; the two men moved their feet out of his way. They paid him no attention but talked to each other in low, urgent voices.

Out of the window on his left Amurao could see the white coral beaches of an island. Green hills were studded with pink stuccoed houses and he recognized where they were – Curaçao, the largest of the ABC Islands or Netherlands Antilles, forty-four miles off the coast of South America. On their way to the offshore oil refinery at the other end of the island.

Working his way around the room, he felt a change in the throbbing of the ship's engines. They were turning. He looked up. The captain was gripping the semicircular metal steering column that rose from the centre of the control panel, turning it hard left.

Out of the window the view had changed. They had come a lot closer to the island.

Amurao stopped mopping.

The captain nodded at his colleague. His second-in-command grasped the big lever in the floor and pushed it forwards all the way. A buzzer sounded and the eight-cylinder engines far below responded like a huge jet. The propeller bit into the dark sea, driving the great ship on.

On the radar screen, an amber bar swept around like a second hand, picking out the glowing outline of the coast. With each revolution the coastline was moving closer. A stopwatch counting down to disaster . . .

1

MAGIC WORLD

The eel's jaws were big enough to encircle Li's entire body. As the creature yawned towards her in the water she glimpsed three vicious sets of teeth and two round eyes, orange and yellow psychedelic discs with inky black pupils. She could hear nothing but the rasp of her own breath in her aqualung and the steady rumble of bubbles as she exhaled through her regulator. The hideous prehistoric face lunged towards her in eerie silence, its jaws snapping open and shut like an alligator.

Li tumbled out of the way and the eel slid

harmlessly past, still snapping its jaws. It wasn't trying to attack her; this was how it breathed. She curled around in the water, lifted her video camera to her masked face and filmed it – the pointed, primitive face like a sea-going snake, bubbles escaping through small holes in its head. The body was nearly three metres long from pointed snout to arrow-like tail and as thick as a telegraph pole.

Up above her on the surface was the *Fathom Sprite*, the eight-metre motorboat they had hired, tethered and flying a blue-and-white flag to show there were divers in the area. She and the four other members of Alpha Force had come to the Fathoms Dive Centre in Curaçao to train in advanced diving techniques. For now, their first afternoon, they were enjoying the island's coral reef and reminding themselves of the basic rules of diving.

The coral reef was vast, an underwater cliff that stretched down for ever. It was far too deep to explore with basic scuba equipment, so rule number one was to make sure you knew how far down you'd gone. As Li swam around she kept a close eye on the dive computer on her wrist to check that she never went deeper than thirty metres. Later in the week, with different equipment and more training, she hoped they'd be able to go deeper.

So far, though, there was so much to see that Li didn't feel shortchanged. Her Anglo-Chinese parents were naturalists and she had inherited their love of the natural world. She hung in front of the wall, the gentle current fanning her black hair out in a rippling flame behind her. 'Wall' somehow seemed the wrong word. It looked like a bluish, brownish rockery full of plants and weeds, but the coral was actually all made of living animals. She swept her torch over it and the muted colours became bushes of bright red, yellow and jewel-like purples. There were delicate white structures that looked like the vein structures of giant leaves. In between them all were pale ripples of hard corals like human brains. The textures looked so alien and beautiful she wanted to touch them, but some of them were poisonous. In any case, the whole reef was a conservation area and divers were forbidden to touch anything in case they upset the ecosystem.

Diving this reef was like being a bird. She could

hover, or move up and down effortlessly with a flick of her fins. With the endless deep blue below her, it was like dreams she'd had of being able to fly. A talented gymnast, martial artist and climber, Li adored anything that felt like defying gravity.

Strange, though. It was no longer as quiet as it had been. As well as the gentle sound of her own breathing she could now hear a deep sort of rumbling sound, like very muffled thunder. She couldn't say when it had started, but she was sure it hadn't always been that loud.

Li checked her luminous watch. They had been underwater for about ten minutes. Diving rule number two was to keep an eye on how long you'd been down because you didn't want to run out of air. But Li felt like she could spend for ever down there.

All the time she had been keeping track of the others. They all carried torches so it was easy to see where they were. That was diving rule number three – don't go off on your own. You always had a dive-buddy to look out for you. Today, she had two – Paulo and Alex. Time to film them for a while, she thought.

She picked Paulo out easily by his powerful build and dark wavy hair billowing up in a soft halo. He was above her, suspended in a ring of silvery fish, as though he had charmed them out of the reefs. He saw Li pointing the camera up at him and gave a big, theatrical flourish with his hand. The fish parted in a tunnel. He withdrew it again and they closed around him like a giant rotating lampshade.

Typical Paulo, thought Li. He had grown up on a ranch in Argentina and was supremely confident with animals. Here he was, orchestrating the movements of at least two hundred fish. Any minute now he's going to give a big show-off grin and then his regulator will fall out of his mouth. Or he'll breathe through his nose. She made sure she got a close-up of his bouffant hair; that would make amusing viewing later.

Alex had been watching. He swam past Li, his blond hair rippling around his face, and copied Paulo's flamboyant gesture. Li filmed him, knowing what no-nonsense Northumbrian Alex would be saying about Paulo if his dive equipment allowed him to speak: 'posing as usual'. As he swam off Li took a few quick frames of Alex's billowy hair too.

Amber and Hex were easy to spot. Hex's fins were pale in the blue light, edged with black like a dangerous fish; Amber's were as black as her skin, making her already long legs impossibly sleek. They were swimming as a pair at ninety degrees to the coral wall, as though they had forgotten which way was up. Several fish seemed to have been fooled too and were swimming along beside them. To anyone who knew them they would seem unlikely dive-buddies – Amber, a privileged rich girl from America, and Hex, a computer hacker from a rough part of London – but the two had clicked. Now they swam closer to the coral wall, changing direction in sync like a pair of seahorses, bubbles rising from their masked faces like thought clouds. Both had close-cropped short hair – no potential there, Li thought, for embarrassing underwater hairstyle videos.

Amber poked Hex in the back as they swam along. He whirled in the water looking for his attacker, obviously imagining sharks. Amber hovered beside him, the tubes on her air tank quivering and bubbles shooting fast out of her regulator. So that was what someone looked like when they laughed in scuba gear, Li thought. Hex reached across to poke Amber in return and she scooted gracefully away. He gave chase. And still they swam as though the world had been turned on its side.

That was another of the rules of diving; always know which direction you're going in. It was easy to become disorientated in the water. On night dives particularly, you might think you were surfacing but in fact be swimming endlessly down. All five members of Alpha Force were well trained in navigation techniques. Sometimes their lives had depended on it.

Alex came into Li's viewfinder again, now swimming alongside a gigantic grouper fish. It was the size of a small car and made him look as though he had swallowed a shrinking potion. In the light from her torch she could see that the fish was orangey red with mottled pale lines. The perfect portrait of Alex. His father was in the SAS and Alex seemed to have found the one sea creature that wore desert-issue camouflage.

The big fish fluttered its tail and darted away. Alex stopped and looked around, puzzled.

Li realized the booming sound was much louder. Paulo's cloak of silver fish suddenly deserted him and Hex and Amber stopped too. For a moment the five friends looked around at each other questioningly, treading water. The sound had been growing and growing but was now so loud that they could no longer hear their own breathing.

Where was it coming from? When they looked around, all they could see was wide blue sea and the flowing vertical garden.

Then a huge shape loomed over them in the water like a thundercloud. An enormous ship. It rumbled over them, the throbbing of its engines resounding on every metal item in their kit. Paulo, Alex and Hex were pointing up at it, frantically miming a movie camera to Li. They wanted her to video it. What was it with boys and machines? she thought – but to humour them she lifted the camera. A red light flashed. Out of batteries.

The rear of the boat finally came into view, its mighty propeller spinning in a round opening as tall as a man. The sea behind it boiled into tiny white bubbles. Then the sunlight poured back into the sea again.

They looked at the retreating shadow, then Alex tapped his watch. Time to go. They turned and swam upwards. At the top of the wall was a sandy shelf, the start of the shallow waters near the island. The noise was receding but it was still loud, the boom of the ship's engines like the throbbing of a great heart.

They began to swim back to their boat, the current from the ship's wake pulling them along. Then, like a shoal of fish, they all stopped suddenly. Twenty metres away in the water they should have seen a black diagonal thread – the anchor line. Instead the thread was waving loose in the water.

They swam over to it. The anchor line had snapped and was curling in the current like a slender eel.

Alex swam upwards. As he surfaced he found himself bobbing around like a cork. The sea was still choppy from the passing ship. But he wasn't the only thing being tossed around. Where the boat should have been the water was scattered with debris. The *Fathom Sprite* had been hit – and shattered like a toy.

The tanker was already a good distance away, heading for the white coral cliffs of the island.

Li and the others came up in a rumble of bubbles, exploding onto the surface as though they were coming to the boil. They looked around at the bobbing white pieces of their boat, too stunned even to take their masks off. Paulo felt something knock into him – the boat's engine, nudging at his back like a questing fish.

'Mind out!' Amber's shrill voice pulled them back to practicalities. Her regulator was dangling over one shoulder and she was holding onto a yellow object like a folded canvas pillow. She found the ripcord and pulled. There was a hiss of compressed air and it inflated, unfolding to three times its size.

Li saw the life raft about to engulf her and dived out of the way. When she broke the surface again the first thing she saw was the tanker. It was running, at full speed, into the white cliffs.

The noise was terrible – a dull metallic boom,

then the sound of grinding metal, on and on like it was in slow motion. Everyone froze: Amber, holding onto the ropes on the raft, pulling Hex in; Alex, also in the raft, turning to help Paulo up; Li, only her head out of the water. In that moment, her vision became a split screen, her mask half submerged, half out in the air. Below was the tranquil world of rippling blue with black stingrays banking and turning like cloaks. Above were the clouds, the tropical island – and a huge, rust-spattered tanker full of thick black oil subsiding into the sea . . .

2

Shock

Alex flopped back in the raft, dropped his regulator out of his mouth and took his mask off. He left them where they fell dangling around his neck. 'I'm not going to take this lot off, guys. In case we all end up in the water again.'

'We shouldn't,' said Amber, 'unless someone does something silly.' Nevertheless, she and the others kept their kit on too. The raft didn't feel nearly as solid as a boat.

Paulo was looking around the raft. It looked like

a large children's paddling pool. 'Does this thing have a radio?'

Amber shook her head. 'No. That went down with the boat.' She unzipped a compartment in the side of the raft and took out two short paddles. 'This is how we're going to get home.' She handed one to Hex, took the other and they began to paddle towards the shore, digging into the water like kayakers.

'Should we see if anyone on the tanker needs help?' said Alex, watching the stricken vessel.

'They've got lifeboats,' said Hex. 'See, they're coming out now.'

As he spoke, a crane swung out from the tanker deck to lower a white boat. They could see small figures peering over the edge as the lifeboat was lowered. No sooner had it hit the water than the ship gave another lurch and the entire stern with its living quarters disappeared beneath the surface, leaving only the communication masts visible. The whirling radar antennae sparked and became still.

Now all they could hear was the gentle splash of oars as Hex and Amber paddled in a slow, steady rhythm. Red pressure marks from the masks framed their eyes, making them look tired. Puddles of water collected on the yellow canvas floor.

'I'll take next turn at paddling,' said Paulo.

'Me too,' said Li. Her voice was subdued.

Alex looked towards the small white-painted jetty in the distance, and the long wooden building behind it that was the dive school. 'What on earth are we going to tell Danny about his boat?'

Nobody answered.

They paddled, steadily but surely. It was barely five minutes since they had surfaced and found their boat gone, but they had taken disaster in their stride.

Alpha Force had learned about survival the hard way when they had been five strangers marooned together on a desert island. By the time rescue arrived they had pulled together into a tight-knit team. The experience had been a turning point in their lives – especially for Amber. She had been getting over the deaths of her parents and had discovered that they had been living secret lives fighting human rights abuses. What the five friends went through on that island had shown them that they also could make a difference to those in trouble.

Now, they had dual lives. During term time they were in far-flung corners of the globe, at school or college, keeping fit in their spare time and improving their individual skills. In the holidays they came together to put it all into practice with some extreme sports and training. Quite often these training sessions had a habit of leading them into more serious challenges.

They heard the dinghy before they saw it, the sound of its engine carrying over the water like the drone of a bee. A small blob was racing out from the shore, a silver dinghy carrying two figures in orange lifejackets.

Alex squinted into the distance, his hands shielding his eyes from the bright sun. 'Hey, the coastguard's out and about.'

'They're coming for us,' said Li.

The dinghy drew up close, its engine cut to idle and a man leaned over to talk to them. He had thinning blond hair and a deep tan from a lifetime spent on boats. His lifejacket was printed with the word COASTGUARD.

'Anyone hurt?'

'No, we're fine,' Alex confirmed.

As he spoke, Paulo greeted the athletic, ebony-skinned figure with the coastguard. 'Hi, Danny,' he said with his warmest smile. Danny was the owner of the dive school, a younger man than the coastguard. 'I'm really sorry, but I'm afraid something's happened to the *Fathom Sprite*.'

The others waited in tense silence. The accident had hardly been their fault but they hadn't worked out yet how they would break the news. Paulo, with his usual easy charm, had come straight out with it.

'I guessed,' said Danny. 'When we saw you in this.' His face, normally creased with permanent laugh lines, was grave.

There was a moment of silence as both boats bobbed up and down together on the waves, like horses on a fairground carousel. In the distance, the white lifeboat from the tanker had reached the shore.

The coastguard put his hand on Danny's shoulder. 'You can sue the oil company, Danny,' he said. 'That tanker was going too fast on an unauthorized course. I've got evidence.'

'Evidence?' said Alex.

The coastguard nodded. 'I had a call from a passenger cruiser which was nearly hit by an out-of-control tanker – that tanker. You're lucky you weren't in the boat at the time.' He looked at the raft. 'Do you guys need a ride? We can give you a tow.'

Paulo picked up a paddle. 'Actually,' he said, 'I was quite enjoying this.'

Amber smiled up at the two men. 'I think we're just fine.'

The coastguard gave them a small salute and nodded to Danny. He opened the throttle and they sped away.

Amber tiptoed into the lounge bar and perched on the arm of the sofa next to Hex. She was late because she had had to inject her insulin. As a diabetic, she had to be careful about eating regularly and never forgetting her medication, but she didn't let it cramp her style and was a full and active member of Alpha Force.

The cosy, wood-panelled room was packed. The twenty guests who were staying at the dive centre were there, plus various members of staff. All eyes were on the TV up in the corner. Normally it was only on when there were sporting events and concerts; but today the local news was covering the story of the stricken tanker. On the screen was an aerial picture of the vessel, taken from a helicopter. Badged in one corner with the channel logo, the image changed as the camera circled from the rust-red prow poking out of the water to the tips of the communication masts – all that remained of the stern. Around it, like an ominous shadow, the clear blue water was turning black. Amber swallowed. The oil was already leaking from the ship.

The programme cut back to the studio, where an anchorwoman looked at the camera with a steely eye. '*Those were pictures today of the ArBonCo tanker disaster. I have here in the studio Dr Mara Thomas, Curaçao representative of the environmental group ABC Guardians and a GP at the local medical centre. Mara, how bad is this?*'

The camera panned back to show a strong-jawed Caribbean woman in her forties. '*It's a catastrophe,*' the doctor said. '*It's a very delicate ecosystem out there. The whole community has worked for years to keep the area clean. The reef provides a livelihood for us all – food, tourism, it all depends on it. This oil will kill so much marine and bird life. Imagine what a nuclear war would do to the city – it's like that.*' As she spoke her dark curly hair quivered like wire; although it was held in an antique clip it threatened to escape at any moment.

'Yo, Mara,' called a voice – Danny, his elbows resting on the rough wooden bar top that looked as though it had come from an old galleon. Behind him, gathering dust with the bottles of local rum on the top shelf, were several trophies. 'You tell them what it's doing to us,' he continued.

On the television, a new image had appeared. A man in a grey suit was waiting patiently and the anchorwoman introduced him: '*I have here Piers Hijkoop, legal representative of ArBonCo Oil. Piers, these are strong words. How do you respond to these concerns?*'

The man replied calmly. '*We understand the concerns of the locals and very much regret what has happened. Our experts are already at the scene of the accident. They should be able to contain the spill so that the threat to marine life is minimized.*'

Danny spoke again. 'Looks like it's too late for that.' There was a murmur of agreement from everyone in the room. Alpha Force recognized the man sitting near him: it was the coastguard they had met earlier.

On the screen the anchorwoman asked Piers Hijkoop: '*Any clues as to what caused the crash?*'

'*It's too early to say. We will be examining the black box. As I said, it's a regrettable incident and we're doing all we can.*'

'*Piers Hijkoop, Dr Mara Thomas, thank you very much.*' The anchorwoman turned away from her guests and addressed the camera. '*We'll be bringing you more on the story as and when we get updates. And now on to other news—*'

Danny fired the remote at the screen. It blinked off. For a moment the only noise in the room was the soft lilt of reggae music on the radio.

A woman joined Danny behind the bar and helped herself to some juice from the fridge. Alpha Force recognized her too – Danny's American partner, Lynn, who had been a photographer before they decided to set up Fathoms Dive Centre together. She had helped them settle in when they first arrived.

Amber heard her grumble to Danny: 'Well, Mara didn't get much of a say.'

The coastguard was leaning over the bar now as well, joining in the conversation. 'They won't keep Mara quiet for long.'

Amber was struck by how they spoke – as though they knew Mara personally. Everyone in this community seemed to know each other; they were like one big family. A family on the brink of potential tragedy.

People were heading for the bar and looking for drinks, so Danny and Lynn had to put on their professional faces. Slowly the room was filled with the murmur of conversations.

Alex stood up to give the people at the bar more room. 'Guys, I think we're in the way here. Anyone fancy a breath of fresh air?'

The others nodded. They got up and headed for the row of double doors that led out onto the veranda.

Below was the dive school's private bay, jetty and

beach. The sun was setting, like a bonfire behind the mountains on the west side of the island. Most of the white beach was already in darkness and red-orange light glinted off the waves as they surged and ebbed up and down the beach.

Something caught Li's eye and she went down the wooden steps to the beach. Noticing her body language, the others followed silently and saw what she had seen. Close to, the surface of the water had an iridescent petrol sheen, like oil on the surface of a puddle in a car park. It swirled purple and blue in the light from the setting sun.

Li kneeled down. The sea came all the way up to her feet, then began its retreat, water sinking down between the shards of coral on the beach as it left, winking into bubbles and then into nothing – but not quite nothing. There was now a dark film over the white coral. And a smell.

Hex sniffed. 'Rotten eggs.'

Li stood up. Another wave came and went, leaving another layer of oil.

Paulo caught the expression on her face. 'It's started,' he said.

3

Black Death

The next morning the white beach was black and slimy. Small white mounds of sand appeared like starbursts in a night sky as tiny crabs dug their way out, pushing clean sand to the surface. Dead crabs and molluscs lay strewn around, all coated with glistening black, while others struggled in the slime. It reeked of sulphur.

The five members of Alpha Force stood on the veranda and looked out at the mess. It was even worse than they'd expected.

'What a difference,' said Hex. 'It's obscene.'

'It spreads so fast,' said Paulo.

And still the sea brought more. The clear blue sparkling water was tainted with a rainbow sheen, the white sandpiles from escaping creatures darkening with every wave.

'We had an oil spill once on the beach in Northumberland,' said Alex. 'A tanker ran aground in a storm. There were dead birds everywhere. I thought we'd see dead birds here.'

Li answered his question in a low voice. 'We'll see the birds soon. Give it time. At the moment they'll be trying to clean oil off their feathers, shivering like fury. But the oil will destroy the waterproofing in their feathers so they'll get colder and colder. Then they'll try to eat more but their digestive systems will be irritated by the oil. They'll start burning up their own body tissues to keep warm. And they'll keep trying to clean themselves, and all that oil they're swallowing will poison them. By the time we see them they'll be desperate.'

Amber's eyes were starting to water from the fumes. She rubbed them. 'This stuff is vicious.'

Even the sounds of the landscape were different.

There was the usual steady drone of boats, but also the beat of a helicopter. One came close enough for them to see its tail with the red insignia of ArBonCo Oil. Then it disappeared around the headland towards the tanker.

'I wonder if they really can do anything?' said Alex.

'Why haven't they called us yet?' said Amber. 'Hex, you definitely got through and put us on the list of volunteers?'

'I spoke to them last night,' said Hex. 'In person, not a machine.' He patted his mobile phone on his belt. 'As soon as the call comes, we'll know. They said they were waiting for supplies.'

Li let out a long sigh. 'Surely there must be *something* we can do now.'

Hex shook his head. 'They said no one's to enter the water until the equipment's here. Otherwise we run the risk of spreading the oil further. Plus the tanker's unstable and might explode if any air has got in with the oil.'

Paulo winced. 'Nasty.'

Amber frowned. 'Surely it's seawater in there, if anything?'

'No,' said Hex. 'Not all the tanker's underwater. The containers that aren't might have been holed. It's probably just a precaution.'

'So we just wait?' said Amber.

'Yeah,' said Hex. 'We just wait.'

Alex moved towards the veranda doors. 'I've done enough waiting. Does anyone feel up to some studying? There's lots of diving stuff we could revise.'

Amber thought that whoever had tried to make the dive centre library look like part of an old ship had not realized that most of the walls would be covered in books. Not old leather-bound gold-lettered books either; the diving textbooks were full of modern typefaces and clashing colours. Danny kept the place well stocked with the latest publications.

As the five teenagers sat at the big table, surrounded by books, their sense of time dragging disappeared. Training always put them in a positive frame of mind. It was storing up tools that could be useful for some mission in the future, something that would let them do their job better – or even save their lives or the lives of others. They took training very seriously. For a while they almost forgot about the ruined landscape outside.

Hex kept consulting his palmtop, a state-of-the-art computer that was his pride and joy. He carried it everywhere with him in a belt-mounted pouch. His one complaint about doing so much diving was that he had to leave it behind. But he had managed to put it to good use the previous day, taking notes from an in-depth lecture that Danny had given them on 'the bends', or decompression sickness. If they dived deeper than thirty metres, the weight of the water forced nitrogen from the air they were breathing to dissolve in their blood and joints. They had to be very careful how long they stayed down – and how fast they surfaced – or the dissolved nitrogen would fizz up in their bloodstreams like the gases in a can of drink. The bubbles might burst blood vessels, rupture lungs or even damage nerves. The deeper they dived, the higher the risk. There was a lot of theory to learn before they could dive safely at these depths, and a lot of maths to practise.

Paulo had found a stack of videotapes. 'We ought to look at one of these.' He read off the titles.

'*Nitrogen Narcosis: The Facts*; *Diving Physiology*—'

'We've done those,' chorused Amber and Li.

'How about *Psychological Preparation for Diving*?'

'Done that too,' said Alex.

Hex interrupted as something caught his eye in the book he had in front of him. 'Did you know,' he said, 'that decompression sickness was first observed by Robert Boyle in the seventeenth century? He put a viper in a vessel and increased the pressure—' He put his hand up like a policeman stopping traffic. 'Don't ask me how because it doesn't say. After *de*creasing the pressure he noticed that a bubble formed in the eye of the snake, and it was writhing in pain.'

Li thought that Hex had a certain air of satisfaction when he closed the book. 'That's disgusting,' she said. 'I hope the viper bit him.'

Alex blew his cheeks out. 'I thought all Boyle ever did was write boring old Boyle's Law.'

'Hey, guys,' said Amber. 'This is so weird. We could all be at my school in study period.' She glanced at Hex. 'Except for you. They wouldn't let you in my school.'

'I wouldn't want to come to your school,' rejoined Hex. 'It's just for rich American girls.'

'I think *I'd* like it there,' said Paulo.

'Oh, listen to him,' said Li. 'Mister heartbreaker. If you set foot in a girls' school they'd have you for breakfast.'

Paulo gave her a smouldering look. 'They can have me anytime.' Li picked up her notes and rapped them down on his tanned hand.

'What's your place like, Alex?' Amber asked.

'Oh – so-so,' said Alex. 'Just your usual kind of college. Near the moors. That's what I like about it.'

Paulo read out another title. '*Gas Mixes*. No, we've done that too. *Cliff Diving Championships 2004*.' That one took the wind out of his sails.

'*Cliff Diving Championships 2004*?' Alex repeated.

Paulo looked at the video. It wasn't commercially produced; the label was handwritten in biro. He handed it over to Alex, who was next to the combined TV/video unit, and Alex slotted it into the machine and switched it on. They leaned forward to watch.

The tape started abruptly, panning around a crowd, showing mostly the backs of their heads. The colours were harsh and bright and the sound was hissy but there was the unmistakable air of anticipation, like an audience waiting for a concert. Only they weren't looking at a stage. They were looking at a jagged outline of cliff, about thirty metres up. The camera panned around and showed a rocky headland surrounded by dark blue water. Perched on a lower rock, about halfway up the main cliff, were three figures with score cards. The judges.

A figure appeared on the summit of the cliff, his dark limbs rippling with muscle, looking all the more striking in red trunks. A rustle of expectation went around the crowd and the video zoomed in.

'It's Danny,' said Alex.

Danny's face was lost in concentration, hardly registering the spectators below. Not a muscle in his body moved and gradually his stillness hushed the crowd. He took a step forwards and sprang into the air, twisting like a cat, then tumbling into one back somersault, then another. The camera followed him down, the cliff behind him a blur. Even after doing all that he still had time to straighten up and hit the water feet first.

The camera focused on the water where he had gone in, the crowd now utterly silent. Then Danny burst to the surface, arms held high in triumph and the audience went wild.

Amber was the first to find her voice. 'Wow,' was all she could manage.

Paulo said, 'He must have hit that water at about a hundred k per hour. How could anyone do that and survive?'

The judges on their rock held up a row of numbers. Danny had scored three perfect tens.

'Well, that explains what all the trophies in the bar are,' said Alex.

On the screen, Danny had disappeared behind a group of fans, who were all trying to hug him as he got out of the pool.

'And this guy's our technical diving teacher?' said Amber. 'We are not worthy.'

On the screen, the fans' adulation of Danny continued. 'I feel like hugging him too,' said Li.

Paulo gave her a sidelong glance. 'I wonder how I can learn to dive like that.'

'I don't think I'd fancy the little trunks,' said Alex.

Another contestant was ready on the cliff top. Again the crowd whistled and cheered a greeting, then fell silent. The diver leaped into the air, his arms stretched out wide, then he tucked all his limbs in and performed a double somersault.

They could see what was going to happen. He hadn't timed it right. The five friends gasped as he hit the water at an angle. The dark pool swallowed him and bounced him up; they caught a glimpse of a limp figure sprawling on the surface and heard a shriek from the crowd, then Danny's face was close to the camera, pulling his finger across his throat. *Cut*, he mouthed. The picture went to snowy silence.

Alex clicked the video off and ejected the tape.

'Ouch,' said Hex.

'That would be like hitting concrete,' said Paulo.

Hex's phone suddenly vibrated on his waistband. He whipped it out. 'Hi, Danny.' He listened and nodded, then said, 'OK,' and cut the connection.

'Are we off?' said Alex.

Hex stood up and started to tidy the books. 'We need to get full-length wetsuits and dive boots,' he said. 'Danny's teaching at Stormy Point and wants us to meet him there.'

Stormy Point was a collection of jagged rocks at the corner of the bay. Now the five friends saw it in a new light, as a series of natural diving platforms. Danny, in cut-off shorts and Nike T-shirt, was sitting at the bottom on a plateau overlooking a pool of deep water, his long, lean frame folded up in a cross-legged position. A small, muscular guy was climbing up to one of the outcrops. The pool was purpose-built, cemented off from the sea, its water pale blue like a swimming pool. It was clean and clear, as the sea had been before the oil put sinister rainbows on its surface.

Danny waved to the five friends as they approached across the veranda. They were wearing their wetsuits, unzipped to the waist because of the heat.

'The clean-up guys are on their way by helicopter,' said Danny. 'Of course, they would have to be late.

We didn't start the lesson because we thought they were going to show up earlier. This is Carl, by the way.'

The figure climbing up to one of the outcrops turned and waved, then resumed his climb. He was blond and tanned; Alpha Force recognized him as one of the guests in the bar the previous night.

Danny called up to him. 'No, not off that one. The same one as before.'

Carl called back. 'But I've done that one.'

'Do it again,' called Danny. 'It's six metres, plenty high enough.'

'But I can do twenty metres.'

'Get six metres right before you go any higher,' Danny replied.

Carl came down to the six-metre platform. Having seen the master at work, Alpha Force watched with keen interest. In the distance, the familiar beat of a helicopter sounded. They all looked up and saw the red shape and its steady flashing lights, one at the front and one on the tail. But it was still a long way away.

Carl went to the edge, looked down, took a deep

breath, leaped out and made his body stiff and straight like a soldier standing to attention. Moments later he splashed into the pool feet first, then surfaced, spitting out water.

'Rubbish,' said Danny. 'You did it again. Keep your legs together.'

Carl heaved himself out and stomped back up.

Paulo was looking towards the helicopter. It bore a red insignia. 'That's ArBonCo,' he said. 'Should only be a couple of minutes.'

Carl whizzed down into the water again.

'Awful,' called Danny as he came up. Carl glared at him.

Li felt for Carl. 'Sometimes it's hard to master a new move,' she said. She had to raise her voice a little; the helicopter was definitely drawing closer.

Danny nodded. 'This is much harder than it looks. Carl's actually quite good. He's been taking lessons for a while. But he lets the wave pull his legs apart. If he did that at twenty metres he'd be torn in half.'

'We saw your video,' shouted Amber. 'Very impressive.'

Danny leaned over and shouted his reply over the noise of the helicopter. 'Then you saw what happened after my dive. That guy didn't walk for five months.'

Carl dived again. This time Danny gave him a thumbs-up as he surfaced. 'Nearly.' As the helicopter descended down onto the road behind the dive centre, he pointed up to the six-metre platform again.

Danny could see that the five members of Alpha Force were fascinated by the cliff diving. He beckoned to them. They put their heads close to him so they could hear what he had to say over the noise. 'Don't – you – try – this,' he shouted slowly and emphatically. 'Here' – he pointed to the pool – 'it's easy. I built it. If you jump into a rock pool out in the bay it might not be deep enough or there could be rocks you can't see.' He gestured at the sea with its shimmering oily surface. 'Especially now.' They all nodded but Danny continued to look at them earnestly. 'I've seen divers *killed*,' he emphasized. The helicopter lifted off again and headed for the hills.

Carl dived again and surfaced. This time Danny was clearly pleased. Two thumbs-ups.

A man in red ArBonCo Oil overalls was walking briskly down the beach towards them. By the time he reached them the heli had gone far enough away so they could talk in normal voices again. He went up to Danny. 'Sorry I'm late. Mr Martino?'

Danny nodded.

'You've got the jet skis?'

Danny gestured towards the jetty. 'They're ready and waiting in the boat.'

The man looked at Alpha Force. 'And you're the volunteers? Let me explain what you need to do.'

4

Damage Control

Danny steered the *Fathom Sprinter* out of the bay. She was white like her sister *Fathom Sprite*, but bigger and more powerful, with enough room for a dozen divers in full kit. On the back was a winch and in place of the central bench stood three jet skis like a row of sea-going motorbikes. Carl had come along too, orange shorts over his black swimming trunks and flip-flops on his feet.

They were heading for two tugboats bearing the red and white ArBonCo logo, anchored about 500 metres away from the shore. Two more boats bearing the logos of other dive centres were also heading that way, also with jet skis on the back.

Li touched Paulo's arm. She was looking back at the headland where the tanker lay. Its deck rose like a gentle ramp out of the water, red with anti-rust paint. She shook her head slowly. 'What's that done to the coral reef?'

Paulo had a question of his own. 'I wonder why it went down at the stern?' he asked. 'I would have expected it to go down at the bow, where it crashed.'

Danny was holding a pair of binoculars in one hand, looking through them at the tanker. 'It's deep there but there are rocks near the surface. Easy to get holed. I checked it out as a dive site because that headland's about twenty-five metres high.'

'Anything to see?' said Alex.

Danny lowered the binoculars. His brown eyes squinted into the sun. 'I'm looking for white streaks where that thing wrecked my boat.' He saw several faces look at him with acute embarrassment and clapped Alex on the back. 'I'm not going to let you forget that in a hurry,' he grinned. He handed Alex the tiller. 'Here, look after this while I put my gear on.'

Alex gulped. 'Are you sure?' But Danny hadn't heard. The others relaxed. Alex decided they must be forgiven. Still, he made sure to be very, very careful.

Paulo's jet ski was first off the *Fathom Sprinter* and the moment the hull touched the water, he gunned the throttle. On the back, Li gasped and grabbed his waist as they streaked away at its top speed of 60 kph. She wasn't completely taken by surprise because she knew he'd do that. Paulo loved any machine, particularly ones you could sit on – or in.

Back by the ArBonCo tugs, the other boats were unloading the rest of the jet skis – two more from the *Sprinter* and two groups from the other dive schools. All the riders were dressed from head to toe in neoprene dive gear: hoods, full-length suits, gloves and boots, to protect their skin from oil splashes. In the *Fathom Sprinter*, Carl, still in his shorts and flip-flops, winched the crane back in.

Paulo steered back towards the group and cut the

engine so it idled. Amber and Hex were on another jet ski, with Alex and Danny on the third. In the tugs were enormous coils of pink and yellow foam, like swiss rolls. The tugs manoeuvred so that they were facing in opposite sections, like two people about to fight a duel, then started to move apart. As they did so, a figure in the back of each tug started to unroll the lengths of foam and feed them into the water. These would form long absorbent barriers – sorbent booms – to stop the oil spreading.

Soon, two long lengths of absorbent foam were drifting in the water, attached to the boats like long tails, one pink, one yellow.

Now for the tricky bit. The teams on the jet skis had to position the barriers. The booms were 100 metres long and if they didn't guide them, they would drift, either to where the water was rougher or inwards towards the oily mess. Either way, instead of containing the oil they would spread it out even further.

The Fathoms Dive Centre jet skis took the pink half of the boom. The other two dive schools went for the yellow one.

Paulo led the way. He took the jet ski two thirds of the way along the boom, then stopped. Behind him, Li leaned over, picked it up out of the water, hoisted it over Paulo's shoulder and grasped it firmly under her arm. Acting smoothly as a team, Hex and Amber, Alex and Danny also moved into position and did the same until they were all carrying the boom behind the moving tug like a giant worm.

It was harder than it looked, thought Alex, at the back. The boom was slippery because of the oil and awkward to hold. His arm could barely reach around it. He could see why you needed a passenger on the back whose sole job was to hold it. They were like ants trying to pick up a huge stick of candy – candy that smelled of sulphur and fumes. Then he glanced across at the other tug and realized they weren't doing too badly at all.

The other team of jet skis was in chaos. Instead of spreading out they were all trying to pick up the boom at the same point. Alex couldn't believe how disorganized they were. As he watched, one of them tried to copy what Alpha Force were doing and put the boom over the shoulder of the driver in front.

But he didn't warn him and the next minute the jet ski toppled them both into the water. For a moment Alex wondered how they could create such a shambles. Then he caught himself. Not everyone knew how to pull together as a team. Alpha Force had been together for so long now that they took their teamwork for granted.

Paulo and Hex kept their eyes on the tug, matching its speed. It slowed and stopped and so did they. Danny did too, Alex noted gratefully.

The figure in the back of the tug turned to Paulo and put a hand up. *Stay there*. Smoothly as a shoal of fish, the three jet skis stopped and idled, rising and falling in rhythm with the waves. The man on the boat took a green fluorescent buoy like a beach ball out of the boat, fixed a weighted anchor to it and attached his end of the boom to the buoy. He looked up at his row of helpers and indicated to them to lower the boom.

Li turned and looked behind her, checking Amber had seen. Amber turned and checked for Alex. Together they lowered the foam boom into the water. That was it – job done.

Now all they had to do was wait until the other half of the boom was positioned, join the two together, and the barrier was up.

But the other half didn't seem to be doing so well.

The team with the other boat had managed to pick up the boom but the jet skis moved off at different times and the boom knocked half of them into the water. As they struggled to get back on, the boom snaked out and away into the open sea.

Paulo and Li pulled up next to Hex and Amber. The two machines bobbed up and down in tandem.

'The yellow team need help,' said Paulo. 'If that boom comes over this way they'll do more harm than good.'

Amber nodded. 'Lead on, cowboy.'

Paulo revved the engine and his jet ski shot away, with Li's hair flowing out behind. Hex opened the throttle and shot after him; Amber let out a whoop of joy. The four of them disappeared in a triumphant wash of spray, the engines letting out a satisfying, deep–throated roar.

Danny and Alex, still holding the end of the pink boom, watched them. 'Any excuse,' said Danny.

A jet ski from the other team was heading out after the errant boom, but soon gave up as Paulo and Hex overtook them, Paulo going for the end and Hex for the middle.

As they reached the boom and cut the engines to idle, the girls on the back leaned over and reached out.

And missed. The sea was much choppier out here. The jet skis were rising and falling like surfboards.

Li leaned close to Paulo's ear. 'I can't reach it. Go closer.'

Paulo opened the throttle a little way. He found himself going backwards.

'Other way, idiot,' cried Li.

Paulo thought he had been going the other way, but the current threw him towards Hex and Amber instead. He caught a snatch of them arguing.

'Amber, just grab the big yellow thing.'

'You do it if it's so easy.'

Alex and Danny, still holding onto the end of the boom, could only watch. 'Do they normally use volunteers for this sort of thing?' said Alex.

'When they phoned me they said anyone could

do it,' replied Danny. 'But it looks quite rough out there today.'

'Why don't they use boats?' said Alex.

'They said boats weren't manoeuvrable enough so it had to be jet skis,' said Danny.

The other jet ski riders just sat watching, bobbing up and down like ducks on a choppy lake.

Amber suddenly got it. Years of sailing had given her a feel for waves and currents and she suddenly understood what they needed to do. She yelled in Hex's ear, 'Let me drive.'

'Don't be daft,' said Hex. 'Just tell me what to do.'

But it was a question of feel; not something Amber could explain. She reached around Hex, grasped the handlebars and twisted. 'Full speed ahead,' she yelled.

Hex had to trust her. He opened the throttle as far as it would go. Amber took the jet ski hard sideways, almost in a skid, then leaned down like a jousting knight, scooped up the boom and sat up, triumphant at last.

Paulo and Li had been watching. 'Hey,' said Li. 'They've got some good moves.'

Paulo realized where he had been going wrong. He needed to come in fast and at an angle. Amber had studied the current and worked with it. Paulo gunned the engine. Li was ready. She grabbed the boom, flipped it up and moments later it was resting over their shoulders, tamed.

Together the four riders brought the end of the other boom back to Alex and Danny. From the watchers on the other skis came a polite round of applause. While one tugboat anchored the boom with a buoy, the second chugged into the middle, where Amber and Li held up the other two ends. Two more weighted buoys joined them together and secured them and that was it. The bay and the leaking tanker were now surrounded by 200 metres of sorbent boom.

The *Fathom Sprinter* rode the waves, heading back towards the shore. Oily water collected in puddles on the white floor as the six jet skiers peeled off their dive clothing.

The beach ahead was edged with black instead of white. A pair of figures in red ArBonCo overalls and full-face masks were walking down the cliff, carrying backpacks and hoses. They looked like they were clearing up a radioactive spill.

'What on earth are they doing?' said Amber.

'The next stage,' said Carl. 'They're either going to squirt the oil back into the sea or coat the beach with detergent so the oil starts to break up.'

'You sound as if you know about this sort of thing, Carl,' said Amber.

'I'm doing a master's degree in marine biology in Canada,' replied Carl. 'I've seen all this before.'

Li was looking at the small red figures with their hoses. 'Detergent,' she repeated. 'That's just more pollution. Do these guys have a clue what they're doing?' She gestured back at the sherbet-coloured boom behind them. 'That was a fiasco. And it's just floating there with two buoys in the middle of the sea – it's not attached to anything.'

'They calculate the position according to the currents and winds,' said Carl. 'That's the furthest the oil will go. Not much will get around the sides and if it does it's not enough to do any harm.'

Danny, at the tiller, had been quiet. Now he spoke. 'I'm going to send you guys home.'

As one, Alpha Force said, 'We're staying.'

'Me too,' added Carl.

'But you came for a holiday,' said Danny. 'We can't give you a holiday.'

'We came to learn technical diving,' insisted Alex. 'We can still do that.'

'And,' said Amber, 'we want to help.'

The mobile on the car dashboard began playing Mike Oldfield's *Tubular Bells*. The driver hit ANSWER before it had got through the first bar and rested his hand back on the leather gear lever, waiting for the traffic lights to change. It was a top-of-the-range BMW, the interior a luxurious oasis of tan-coloured leather.

He snapped a greeting. 'Yes?'

The caller was equally abrupt. Either he didn't like to mess about with pleasantries or he was short of time. 'I thought you said the ship would blow up. It hasn't. It's just sitting there. I keep seeing it on every news programme.' The phone made the voice sound tinny and petulant.

The lights changed and the driver accelerated,

swinging past an elderly brown Vauxhall. 'I thought it would blow up too. They said these things are unpredictable. It's highly unstable. It could go at any minute.'

'Unstable or not, people might go in there and snoop around.'

The driver blistered through the gears up to fourth. The engine calmed and settled to cruise. 'It will be all right. Nobody's going to snoop around.'

'You'd better do something to make sure they don't,' squawked the voice. There was a click.

The driver stabbed at the button to cut the connection and glared at the phone for a moment.

On his right was the TV company. He swung the car in through the gates.

5

Birds

'*May I just say first of all how much we regret the incident*,' said the figure on TV. He looked like a standard executive – suit, tie, clean-shaven and neatly groomed. A caption on the screen said his name was Neil Hearst, CEO of ArBonCo Oil.

Watching the news in the bar was becoming a new ritual. But tonight the audience was smaller – just Carl, Alpha Force, Danny and Lynn.

Lynn gave a derisive splutter. 'And you'll regret the bill you're going to get for all the guests I've had to refund. Plus the cost of our boat.'

On the screen Neil Hearst said, '*We have now surrounded the site. There shouldn't be any further damage.*'

Danny snorted. 'Look at that fat twit in his striped shirt. He couldn't care less.'

Amber wouldn't have put it quite that way, but she had to agree there was a certain insincerity about the man. She glanced at the others. They clearly felt the same.

The phone rang. Danny answered, one eye still on the screen. 'Yes? Oh hi. Greg. Yeah, we're watching it too.'

'Hi, Greg,' Lynn called across. 'I thought he was on duty tonight,' she added. She leaned across to Li. 'Greg's the coastguard,' she explained.

On the TV, Neil Hearst was looking earnest. '*I'm a sailing man myself, so I'm counting the cost personally as well.*'

Danny snorted into the phone. 'Greg, did you hear that? He's saying he can't go out and play in his posh yacht so that means he understands.' Then Greg must have said something important because Danny took his eyes off the screen and concentrated on the call.

The interviewer was saying, '*I understand the captain of the tanker is receiving medical care, is that right?*'

'*Yes,*' said Neil Hearst. '*He is suffering from stress and is taking sick leave.*'

Danny put the receiver down. The interviewer wrapped up and moved on to another story.

Lynn hit the OFF button and turned to look at Danny. 'What did Greg say?'

Danny looked tired. 'They've cordoned off the cliff: we can't go near it because the impact might have made it unstable. Plus the tanker might explode because of air mixing with gases from the oil. His daughter's asthma has flared up because of all these fumes and he had to rush her to the medical centre. And the Fisheries Authority has introduced a fishing ban.'

Carl's expression was pained. 'Oh – and I was looking forward to some more of your delicious flying fish, Lynn.'

'Why don't they ban breathing while they're at it,' said Lynn, 'since that's now bad for us.' She looked at the six remaining guests. 'Honestly, guys, I don't know how you can still stand it here.'

The five friends kept thinking about Lynn's words. When they woke up the next morning the air still smelled of the rotten sulphur of the oil, but it had a new, astringent note. They could smell it all the time they were in the library, quizzing Danny about gas mixtures for different levels of diving while they waited to hear how they could help. Everywhere was quiet; instead of the constant cries of seabirds, there was just silence. When volunteers were once again summoned to help with the clean-up, they put on wetsuits and went back out to the beach. That was when they got their biggest shock.

The beach looked like industrial waste ground. Men in red overalls, gloves, masks and rubber boots were walking up and down, spraying it with chemicals from tanks on their backs. It no longer looked like sand; it looked like glossy tar. Between their footprints, the blackened corpses of birds struggled and twitched, or had given up the fight and were lying still.

An oil-covered bird staggered onto the beach and toppled over, its proud plumage sticking out in oily spikes and only its eyes looking normal. Paulo kneeled to look at it. A black pattern of scum swirled around the small depression its body had made, the liquid trickling down the shore and into the sea like tears. The bird blinked as the chemicals touched its eyes.

A busy-looking man in red overalls beckoned them over to a crate and gave them rubber gloves and face masks. Then it was time to start digging the birds out of the slimy sand.

Some locals were already at work, carefully picking up bird after bird. Hex never forgot the moment he touched his first one. Although he wore gloves he could feel the oiled texture of its feathers and the sharp lines of its bones through its skin. He cupped his hands and picked it up – and it twitched. Hex stopped and stared at it, stunned. He had never held a live bird in his hands before. And if this one hadn't been in such a desperate state he wouldn't have been able to hold it.

On the veranda was a trestle table, where a vet stood writing on a clipboard. Hex hurried up there, his feet slipping in the wet, slimy sand. The bird's heart beat like a frantic pump beneath his fingers. By the trestle table was a large basket full of blackened dead birds. It looked like a sick joke. The vet stood over them, her expression weary.

Hex held out the creature cradled in his hands. 'This one's alive.'

The vet carefully took the bird from him. Just touching the emaciated body told her enough. 'I'm afraid there's nothing we can do. She's poisoned. I'll put her to sleep.' She didn't even look at Hex as she spoke; she had obviously done this numerous times already.

Hex watched the vet take the bird to the end of the table. There was a small folding screen arranged on it, like curtained screens in a hospital. He couldn't see what the vet did next and he didn't want to, but he was struck by how carefully and tenderly she treated the bird. He looked at the other locals, working slowly and silently, then at Amber, kneeling down, excavating a bird with the utmost care. Paulo's expressive face showed all the horror he was feeling. Alex's and Li's faces were blank; they were locked in their own private worlds. Lynn, Danny and Carl were there too, digging in a silent line. Many of the other volunteers he didn't know, but one he recognized very well. He couldn't mistake the wild hair – Mara Thomas, the doctor they had seen on TV the other night.

Every hour they needed a break. Despite their masks the fumes made them nauseous and the full-length wetsuits were hot in the bright sunshine. The workers sat on the veranda, gloves off, masks down, wetsuits unzipped, gulping down water.

Mara pulled bottles of Evian out of an ice bucket and handed them around. 'I saw the Rastafarians come down this morning to fish. The Ministry of Fisheries has taped off their spot near the clinic.' She sighed, then leaned across to Li and touched her on the arm. 'Excuse me, dear, I'd wash that off quickly if I were you. I've got patients in my clinic with nasty rashes.' She pointed to the back of Li's neck.

Paulo, next to her, saw a streak of oil like black paint on Li's golden skin. 'You've got a smear of oil. Hold still.' There was a tray of wet wipes on the veranda. He tore one out of its wrapper.

'Mara's our local doctor,' said Lynn as Paulo moved Li's plait aside and dabbed at her neck. 'Have you met her?'

Li nodded a greeting at Mara, then turned to glare at Paulo. 'Don't scrub, you'll drive it into my skin.'

Paulo paused. 'It's not coming off.'

Mara put down her water and moved over to Li. 'Yes it will. Give that here.' She put out her hand and Paulo handed her the wet wipe. She began to stroke the area of oil. Then she looked at it, puzzled. The dark oil smudge hadn't moved. 'Funny,' she said. She held up Li's plait to Paulo. 'Here, can you hold this out of the way?'

Li swayed as Mara scrubbed hard. 'Stop looking like you've been proved right,' she said crossly to Paulo.

'It's not usually as sticky as this,' said Mara.

Carl came and sat down, pulling the top off a bottle of water and holding it up as if to toast the others. He took a long drink then looked at the bottle thoughtfully. 'Isn't there anything stronger?' He looked around for Danny. 'Where's our barman when we need him?'

Hex sat down next to Carl. 'Have you noticed,' he said, 'that some of the oil is thin but some is like treacle and sticks to your gloves?'

Alex was listening to them. He peeled off his gloves with a snap. 'Yeah, Hex, I've seen that. Weird, isn't it?'

Carl shook his head. 'It's impossible. The tanker was only carrying one type of oil. Heavy heating oils, they said.'

Alex shook out his gloves to turn them the right way out. He showed the streaks to Carl. 'No, look. Here I've got a greasy and pale bit, and here there's a sticky, treacle-like bit.'

Carl frowned. 'May I?' He took the glove and looked at it thoughtfully.

Amber rolled her eyes. 'You boys. You'll be comparing boogers next.'

'Mara,' called Carl, holding out the glove, 'what do you make of this?'

Mara put down the wipe she had been using on Li, took the glove and considered the dirty marks on it.

'That's two types of oil, isn't it?' said Carl.

'It shouldn't be,' said Mara. 'They normally only carry one type.' She held up the glove so that the sunlight glinted off it. The lighter streaks had a pearly sheen, but the dark ones remained dull. 'But some of this looks a lot more refined than the other.'

Amber couldn't see what all the fuss was about. 'So this tanker carried two types of oil. What's the big deal?'

'They don't do that,' said Mara. Her springy curls waved as she shook her head. 'It's not economical.'

'You sound as if you have insider knowledge,' said Alex.

'I worked in petrochemicals a long time ago,' said Mara. 'Before I decided I wanted to be a bit more help to mankind and retrained in medicine.'

'The other oil could be the ship's operating fuel,' said Hex. 'Maybe its tank was ruptured.'

'But then they'd say so, wouldn't they?' said Alex. 'Mara, you're the environmentalist. Have they said anything about ruptured fuel tanks?'

'No,' said Mara. She sat down. When she next spoke, her voice was quiet. 'Carl, are you qualified to dive?'

Carl shook his head. 'No. Why?'

'I want to go and look at the wreck,' she said. 'ABC Guardians have a right to know what's really going on. Never mind, maybe I can twist Danny's arm to come with me.'

'We'll go with you,' said Alex in a low voice.

Mara looked around in surprise. She looked into Alex's eyes. He nodded, answering her unspoken question. She looked at Hex and at Amber.

'We're in,' said Hex. 'And Li and Paulo if you want.'

Mara looked at them earnestly. 'We'll have to go at night. This place is crawling with ArBonCo people during the day. How experienced are you?'

Carl answered. 'Danny tells me they're good divers, Mara,' he said. 'He told me he's been doing lots of advanced stuff with them.'

Mara kept her voice quiet. 'Have you ever done anything like this before? If we're going to get evidence you've got to be very precise about the way you work. No contaminating the site.'

Alex nodded. 'No problem. In fact, it's our speciality.'

6

The Tanker

The sun went down and the Fathoms Dive Centre bar at last looked out over a deserted beach.

Below the surface the water was a deep black, sprinkled with green glitter. Passing fish left bioluminescent trails and the divers could see their companions' fins moving in arcs of sparkling light. Some fish were asleep and hidden, and the reef was alive with starry, spiky invertebrates. Brittlestars held out arms like tinsel, looking for plankton, puffing out yellow-green flashes of light at the intruders. Parrotfish hid in the crevices, cocooned inside bags made of their own mucus. The corals waved their polyps, looking for food. But some were already lifeless.

They swam past a giant anchor, seven metres high, left over from the days when pirates roamed the Caribbean. It was crusted with sponges and corals.

As Li swept the area with her torch she could see bubbles – but not just the air bubbles they were breathing out. These bubbles were golden brown and drifted in the currents like blobs in a lava lamp. Oil.

The divers wore full-length suits with neoprene dive boots under their fins and barrier cream on the exposed parts of their faces. They carried two tanks of air each. On their buoyancy control devices or BCDs – the black lifejackets that acted as a harness for the tanks – they also carried lanyards with spare torches and fluorescent light sticks. Most important was a 'slate' – a piece of plastic like a miniature whiteboard with an attached graphite pencil so that they could communicate underwater.

It took ten minutes to reach the wreck. It was huge, the living quarters like an entire sunken block of flats with the deck stretching away for what seemed like miles. Its straight metal walls were harsh beside the grotto-like surfaces around them.

They split into three groups of two: Paulo went with Li, Amber with Hex and Alex with Mara. Each pair had designated areas to investigate, based on plans of the ship that Hex had downloaded before they set out.

Mara and Alex were assigned the outside, to find the hole where the oil had leaked out.

The hull was nearly as deep as the four-storey structure that sat on top. They swam down to the bottom of it, looking for the hole with their torches. Reaching the stern and swimming around the corner, they saw the propeller. Alex stopped. It was awesome, hanging like a giant fan in the centre of a big metal hole. He could have swum between its blades like a minnow.

The next place they had to look at was the underside. Mara led the way, playing her torch up and down. As they reached the bottom, the water erupted in a cloud of green plankton and Alex felt the tip of a tail lash close to his face. He whipped his torch around. A brawny body swished away –

a moray eel out hunting. He took deep breaths, letting his heart rate come back to normal. It was a timely reminder – night was the time for hunting and creatures that were docile by day were alert and hungry. Even if they couldn't eat you, they could give you a nasty bite.

The heel of the stern rested on the rocky bottom. Scattered around were several broken crowns of coral. Mara signalled to Alex that she had found oil – a floating blob on the coral reef, reflecting her torchlight like an iridescent amoeba.

She had previously given each of them a kit for taking samples – a Ziploc bag on a lanyard, containing bottles and a chinagraph pencil – and Alex now took out one of the bottles, held it out and the blob swam into it as though it were a living creature. He put the lid on and labelled it with a note of the location to show where it had been collected, then zipped up the bag. They'd got their first sample.

They moved to where the hull touched the coral floor, paddling gently along it with their hands so that they stayed close to it. Somewhere there must be a hole where the oil was leaking. They collected more stray blobs – no different from the first – then turned the corner and went to investigate the other side.

That's where they found it. A black void, resting on a jagged spear of rock. Blobs of shiny oil were slipping out like fish streaming out of a cave.

Alex looked round at Mara. She had her sample bottle ready.

Paulo and Li were in the engine rooms. Li was not impressed. It was only an engine, for heaven's sake, although she had to admit it was quite a big one. But just how long was he going to float there looking at it?

Paulo was in a blissful dream. The engine loomed out of the foggy black water, pea-green coloured and as big as a two-storey house. Each part was breathtaking. The pistons were so big they could not be circled by five people holding hands. The fuel valves were the girth of a fat man. On the floor beside the engine was a giant metal lever nearly as tall as Li.

Li swam up close to him, pulled herself upright in the water, cocked her head on one side, folded her arms and mimed tapping her foot. She had forgotten she had a fin on the end and the movement sent her shooting upwards. But as she pushed herself off the roof with her hands and floated back down to Paulo he came out of his dream and beckoned her to move on.

Now they were in a chamber above the rear oil reservoirs. There were three of these chambers in all, running all the way along the tanker like hangars with low ceilings. At various intervals in the floor there were hatches, each closed with a wheel.

They swam up to one. In its door was a gauge that registered empty. Paulo turned the wheel and lifted the hatch. He'd expected a large opening but it was only just big enough for a person to pass through, with a valve and another smaller wheel in the corner. According to Hex's plans, this wheel would lift the inner lid and expose the inside of the tank. But he had no need to look in this one as it was empty and he could risk letting out more contamination in the form of gases or oily residue. What they really needed to do was to establish if one still had something in it or was any different from the others.

Paulo reached for his slate and wrote a note on it which he then showed to Li. *Look at all gauges.*

Making sure they were never more than five metres apart, they investigated the other hatches, floating through the hangar and pausing at each one like fireflies visiting flowers.

Li found a tank whose gauge was in a warning area: PRESSURE LOSS. Could this be the one with the hole? She flashed the torch over the cavernous ceiling to beckon Paulo over.

He turned the wheel to release the inner lid, then opened the hatch. A cluster of oil bubbles rose and Li captured them in a bottle, labelling them clearly.

Paulo shone his torch down into the hole. The oil container was like a cave. He lifted his head out. There was no need to say anything. Li simply zipped up her sample and nodded at him. There might be vital clues inside.

Paulo upended himself and swam in. Li followed.

Hex and Amber floated up a staircase like a pair of ghosts. The living quarters were kitted out for voyages of months at a time. Through an open door they glimpsed a squash court and, in a tiny room above a hallway, a cinema with a pair of film projectors pointing at a small glass window. Amber pointed her torch through the glass, watching the plankton swirl in the beam like particles of dust. Cabins came next, the sheets and blankets and pillows still on the beds, cupboards left open and possessions spilled on the floor – an electric razor; a baseball cap. It all looked so normal, thought Hex – not as if they were under all this water.

They floated through a doorway and found a big, hangar-like room. They swam slowly along the ceiling while below them their torches found a rectangle of turquoise: a swimming pool. Amber suddenly took off at speed, miming front crawl. Hex gave chase, his powerful fins making up the distance easily. They raced to the end of the room, reaching the far side at the same time.

Finally they came to the bridge, its window now looking out into black water. Set into the floor was a giant lever that reminded Amber of a massive version of a car's automatic gearshift. On this, however, the positions were: DEAD SLOW, SLOW,

HALF and FULL AHEAD. It was pushed all the way forward, to FULL AHEAD. Amber looked at it, puzzled. Why would anyone have been doing a speed like that so near to the coast?

Li and Paulo had found a hole in the container wall. The ragged gash and bent metal told the story – it had been ripped open by a sharp rock. No sabotage there.

There was nothing more to see. Time to go back. Paulo gestured towards the hole: *After you.*

He watched Li put her head through. Her air hose bent on the sharp metal. He tapped her urgently on the leg and pointed. She reversed carefully and pointed to the hatch. They'd have to go out the long way – back the way they came in and through the ship.

Li led the way up and put her head through.

And got the shock of her life. A shark loomed above her, a big white blunt-headed torpedo. Its jaw came down like a gangplank and the empty-looking eye looked at her coldly.

She scooted back down to Paulo and mimed

snapping jaws with her hand. They both hurriedly turned their torches so that they pointed downwards. They both knew that sharks were attracted by brightly coloured and shiny objects. Li put her finger to her lips in front of her regulator: *Keep quiet*. Gently, they moved away.

The shark was up in the main chamber. If they went up, it might go for them. It was night and in the shallows – prime hunting territory.

Paulo looked at the hatch. Could they close it from the inside? No. There was no handle.

Li pointed towards the ragged hole.

Paulo didn't like the idea. He looked up. The shark passed overhead again, like a patrolling plane. It was stalking them.

He followed Li to the ragged hole.

They ran their torches over it. It was narrow and the edges were like passing between a pair of blades.

Paulo wrote on his slate: *U 1st. I'll guide*.

Li lined herself up with the opening and started to pull herself through. Paulo gently folded the air hoses away from the sharp edges. He nearly caught his fingers and pulled them out of the way just in time. With a shark nearby, the last thing they needed was blood in the water.

Li got through and swivelled around in the water to look at Paulo. He was much bigger than her. There was no way he could get through with his tanks on.

Paulo watched her. She mimed taking off her tanks. He went cold. Take off his air supply?

Li nodded at him emphatically. He knew she was right. At least it wasn't complicated: just undo the BCD and it all came off as one unit. That meant it was easy to put on again, he told himself.

He looked behind to make sure he didn't damage his regulator hoses.

A big pale blunt head loomed at him out of the dark water. The shark had swum through the hatchway. And was coming for him.

Paulo wriggled free of the BCD, took a giant breath and let the regulator go.

Li saw the shark surge up behind Paulo, attracted by her torch and his beating fins. She grabbed him and hauled him through the opening, as the tanks dropped down inside the tanker with a loud clang.

* * *

Alex and Mara heard a repeated clanging, like a laser-shot through the water. It was coming from the hole. They wasted no time. A diver signalled they were in trouble by banging on their tanks. Whatever had happened? It carried on – *bang, bang* again and again.

Alex powered towards the noise and found Li and Paulo by the hole, sharing Li's air supply. Paulo's entire BCD and tanks were gone; the only part of his dive kit that remained was his mask.

Paulo saw Alex and mimed 'shark', then passed the regulator back to Li. She took long, slow breaths while Paulo kept his mouth tightly closed.

Alex could see Paulo's kit through the hole. The shark was headbutting the tanks against the hull. One moment there was a dull thud, the next a piercing clang as metal drummed on metal. Alex flinched, his ears ringing. Why did it want the tanks? Paulo's torch swung on the end of its lanyard as the shark attacked again.

The torch. Was that what it wanted?

Alex whipped the light stick off his kit and broke the seal to activate it. It glowed bright green in his hand, like a much stronger version of the fluorescent fish. Alex shot it in through the opening.

The shark saw the light and lunged, getting its jaws around it and chewing, the light flashing on and off. Alex concealed his torch in case the shark came after him too. For a moment the inside of the tanker was dark, then he saw the green glow again, surrounded by serrated rows of teeth. The shark's mouth looked smaller now, chewing on the light stick as it swam away. It vanished and appeared again moments later, even further away.

Alex turned to see Hex and Amber powering up to them, heads turning from one to the other as they searched their friends' faces for an explanation.

Paulo scribbled on his slate. If anyone could have penetrated his mask they would have seen an expression of utmost innocence as he turned the slate towards the frantic Hex and Amber.

Knock knock.

7

Cover-up

Carl held two test tubes up to the light. One contained a viscous dark brown liquid. The other contained a lighter brown liquid.

While Danny and Lynn had helped the divers rinse down their gear, Carl had got to work on the samples in the lab in Mara's clinic, next door to the dive centre. Now they were all gathered in the lab, sitting around the workbench waiting for the results. In the background some reggae played softly on a late-night radio programme.

'This,' said Carl, shaking the lighter brown liquid,

'is the oil you collected from the tanker. And this' – he held up the other tube – 'is from samples I took from the dead birds while you were out. These are not the same types of oil. You took samples from all over the tanker, right?'

Mara nodded. 'We went over it with a fine-tooth comb.' She nodded at her dive-buddy, Alex, and at the others. 'These guys were great, really thorough.'

'And nothing was leaking from the engines,' said Paulo. 'I looked at them thoroughly.'

'Very thoroughly,' remarked Li.

'It was research,' protested Paulo.

Mara took the dark tube and sniffed it. 'This isn't engine oil anyway. It's really sludgy. You'd clog up an engine if you tried to put that in it.'

'So something else is leaking out there,' said Amber. 'What?'

'Or something dumping its load?' Mara got up and went to the bench where Carl had been working. She put the test tube in a holder, took a pipette and put a small blob of the oil on a sheet of filter paper.

The five members of Alpha Force looked at her in horror. 'Someone *dumping* oil?' repeated Amber.

Mara lifted the filter paper and held it up to the light to look at the stain. 'Some oil companies do that. They dump a load of oil and pay the fine. It's cheaper than transporting it or repairing a leaky boat to bring it up to standard.'

'That's outrageous,' said Li.

Mara was still looking at her filter paper. 'You know what this looks like to me? A mudslick. It's not like crude oil that's transported in a tanker, it's the sludge you get from exploratory drilling.' She put the piece of filter paper down on the bench. 'I think someone is drilling and the hole is leaking.'

'That's illegal,' said Li firmly. 'Isn't it?'

'Too right it is,' Mara agreed bitterly. 'The government has to give permission for drilling. You need to do environmental checks, consult with the locals—'

Amber interrupted. 'What happens if a company doesn't?'

'They're fined,' said Danny, 'by the Clean Caribbean Consortium.'

'Whatever they're fined,' said Amber darkly, 'I bet

it isn't as much as they could make if they just started drilling at once. How long would it take to get approval through the proper channels?'

'A few years,' said Danny, 'wouldn't it, Mara? They have to go through all sorts of committees and public consultation. It's not just about the environment, it's about people's livelihoods.'

Hex stretched. His back and neck were still aching from digging in the sand. 'Well you can see why they'd just rather get on with making money.'

Carl spluttered, 'You can bet your boots they make money. Even a small field brings in a profit of more than half a million dollars a day.'

Mara frowned. 'I wonder who could be doing this? It can't be ArBonCo. They always seemed to be one of the better oil companies. They always went through the proper channels, consulted properly, listened to the locals. They haven't put the environment in danger before. ABC Guardians have never had any problems with them.'

Amber shrugged. 'I suppose some corporations are just in it for the money.'

Alex brought them back to focus on the task.

'OK, well it seems someone has been trying to drill in secret, and the hole has leaked and given them away.'

'It will be very interesting when they analyse the black box,' said Mara. 'I'll ask about it next time they put me on TV.' She scribbled a note and stuck it to her computer.

'You don't have to,' said Hex. 'Amber and I found the ship was set to full speed when it crashed.'

'And we saw it,' added Li. 'It was going straight for the cliffs. It didn't try to take any evasive action. I think they must have crashed the tanker deliberately to cover up what they're doing with the drilling.'

The room went silent.

Lynn began to talk very fast. 'We've got them. Mara, you can take this to the Clean Caribbean Consortium and maybe they can stop this before it goes any further. I'll get the other dive schools, the restaurants, the hotels and we'll go to the local chamber of commerce—'

'Yes, once they look at the black box—' began Mara.

'Whoa, whoa.' Paulo put up his hands. 'They could still claim it was an accident. They already said on the news that the captain was ill. They'll just say he went loco. We've only got one piece of evidence and that's the two types of oil.'

'Well, we'll take that to them,' said Danny. 'They'll have to take notice if enough of us go—' He stopped.

Amber was shaking her head. 'They can say that's nothing to do with them. Coincidence. We have to *prove* where it came from. And we have to get it soon, before they realize we're on to them.'

Mara spread her hands in exasperation. 'How? It could be anywhere.' She sighed. 'I'll call the Clean Caribbean Consortium in the morning and tell them what we've got.'

The five members of Alpha Force glanced at each other. If Mara presented the evidence too soon the oil company might explain it away and then they'd have lost any chance of making a difference.

Alex took a deep breath. 'Carl, you're from Canada. Do you remember Usher Mining Corp?'

Carl frowned. 'Usher Mining Corporation . . .

Yes! Something about dumping cyanide in the north.'

'I remember that,' said Mara darkly.

Alex said quietly, 'They'd wriggled through every loophole . . . but we got them.'

Mara was looking at Alex with new respect. She nodded quietly. 'Good catch. Daniel Usher was running for governor too, wasn't he?'

Alex returned her gaze enigmatically.

She decided to change the subject. 'If we're really going for it,' she said, 'the best evidence of all would be filmed evidence, and the location of the drill site.'

Amber yawned and stretched. 'Better get some sleep then. We've got a lot of thinking to do tomorrow.'

Hex looked at his watch. 'Today. It's well past midnight.'

Amber gave up the struggle to sleep and opened her eyes. Moonlight streamed into the room. For a moment she expected to be able to float up off the bed around to the wardrobe and then the bathroom.

It was like being back exploring the tanker.

'Li,' she hissed, 'are you awake?'

'Yes.' Li's voice didn't sound at all sleepy. Maybe she'd been lying awake too.

'I've been thinking about how we find the drill site. Can we get any clues from the kind of seabirds that have been washed up? Where their feeding grounds are; where they might have picked up the mudslick?'

Li sat up. 'Hmm. Let me think. Quite a lot of the birds nest and feed on the coast, but some build their nests on the coast and feed in the open water. And some spend the whole time at sea once they're mature . . .'

'Hmm. It was sounding promising until you said that last bit. I just thought that if we found a kind of bird that would never go more than a certain distance from its nest, we might know how far out the slick was.'

Despite Amber's reservations, Li's voice became excited. 'Let's get Carl to check what breeds we've found. That's brilliant, Amber.'

'No, it's not, it's rubbish. Forget it.' Amber turned

over and tried to get comfortable. At least she'd got the idea off her chest. Maybe now she could get some sleep.

'Hex, are you awake?'

'No, he's not, but *I* am,' replied Alex's voice.

'Yes, I'm awake,' said Hex crossly.

'If you were going to drill for oil,' said Paulo, 'you wouldn't just start drilling, would you? I mean, it would be expensive. You'd have to have an idea that you were going to find something.'

'I see what you mean,' said Alex. 'There might have been some sort of survey programme. Which could have been noticed.'

There was a sound of fumbling near Hex's bed. Then his face was lit up by the glow of his palmtop. His fingers rattled over the keys.

'What are you looking up?'

'Oil exploration for complete beginners,' replied Hex. He speed-read off the screen, mumbling odd words. '"Oil forms in certain geological . . . blah blah blah . . ."' He was mumbling faster now. '"Shallow parts of oceans . . . blah blah."'

'How do you do a survey underwater?' Paulo queried. 'Submarine?'

'Aha,' said Hex. 'Listen. "Locations are assessed from a boat by seismic survey. Blah blah blah . . ." Basically they sail up and down and fire soundwaves at the sea bed.'

'We should get Danny to ask Greg if anything like that's been going on,' said Paulo. 'As coastguard, he'd probably know all about who comes and goes in these waters.'

Hex powered down the palmtop and the room was dark once more.

The sound of his mobile playing *Tubular Bells* interrupted Neil Hearst's first latte of the morning. He frowned at the display and answered quickly.

'Simon, I told you not to phone me at work.'

'I've seen the results from the labs. I've had to sit on them. You idiot, you got the wrong kind of oil.'

Hearst took a deep breath and swivelled his chair so that he faced out of the window. His office at the ArBonCo headquarters gave a splendid view of Curaçao's capital, Willemstad. The houses decorated in blue, pink, yellow and green, topped with red tiled roofs and rococo gables like iced gingerbread houses, looked like they had been transplanted from fairytale Amsterdam. He liked them. They were quaint and that made him feel in control. 'Yes, I know. I didn't have much time to set it up.'

'You were paying them. What was the problem?'

'I had to find a captain who wanted to retire. It wasn't just a case of crashing the tanker, I had to find a captain with health problems who wanted to be invalided out. There aren't many of those.'

'You'd better do something about it or the deal's off. That tanker's a mine of evidence.'

There was a click and the connection was cut.

Neil Hearst put the phone in his lap and let out a long, thoughtful sigh.

8

Secret Site

The vet took the bird from Amber and went behind the screen. Amber looked away. Out in the bay the pink and yellow sorbent booms were already dark brown and the air was filled with hissing as the red-suited figures washed the oil down into the water with high-pressure hoses. Amber was beginning to recognize some of the other volunteers now: the guy who delivered the vegetables from the market; some off-duty staff from the medical centre. The whole community was involved in the clean-up.

The hoses stopped and in the silence Amber heard

the chink of instruments and bottles as the vet worked. There was a rasping noise as the bird's oily feathers spasmed against the vet's rubber gloves, like a last-ditch attempt to escape. Then the hoses started again. The vet laid the bird in a black plastic sack.

Amber was about to go back down the beach when she saw Li, Alex and Carl waving to her from inside the bar. She took off her mask and went over to talk to them.

'Did you get anything from Greg?' she asked Alex.

Alex shook his head. 'No records. Only if there had been a mayday call or they'd caused an accident. But—'

There were books lying open on the bar and Amber noticed that some showed maps and others seemed to be ornithology texts. Li grabbed her arm and squeezed. 'Amber, you've cracked it.'

'How?'

'The birds,' said Carl hurriedly. 'We've found a lot of mature tropicbirds. Normally they live way out at sea but they come back to nest – and – get this – they only nest on *remote* cliff faces.'

'Yes?' said Amber.

Carl continued. 'There aren't a lot of those habitats left now, but there's one place in Curaçao where they're protected.'

Alex pulled out the map and pointed to a spot. 'Here.'

Amber looked. He was pointing to an area not far from the tanker. 'But we thought the mudslick came from further out.'

'Yes,' said Li, 'but here's the clever bit. Although these birds have their nests here on the coast, they fly out to hunt. They'll only go out a limited distance to get food.' She pointed to the map. '*That's* where we need to look.'

'Those two have been out there for a couple of hours,' said Alex, indicating Hex and Paulo, who were still outside with the digging party. 'It's time for me and Li to do a bit – but Amber, why don't you join them for a long break on the water . . . ?'

Amber, in shorts and her favourite burgundy bikini, checked that the *Fathom Sprinter* was securely anchored. Paulo and Hex were clicking away at their dive computers. This would be a great opportunity to practise all they had recently learned about decompression. They were going down deep – to sixty metres.

The boys were kitted up in BCDs, each with two large tanks. The dive computers were chunkier and more complex than the dive computers they had been using so far, and the tanks were dull green instead of the normal yellow because the mix of gases for deep diving was different. They wore full-length wetsuits and hoods, not only for protection but also for warmth because they would be spending a lot of time waiting in the water for their bodies to adjust as they came up. The dive computers would give them precise instructions and they had to obey them to the letter.

Despite all they had to remember, the two boys looked excited as they made their calculations. They were the most mathematically adept of the group and were the natural choice to be first to try the activity.

'With decompression we need to stay down ninety minutes in total,' said Paulo. 'So that leaves us with about fifteen minutes to get there and fifteen minutes to video the site.'

'That's not much time to find it,' said Amber. She then wished she hadn't said anything because the look on Hex's face was just a little too smug.

'It isn't if you have to search for the site,' he grinned. 'But if you have a genius who can look up the currents and calculate where the slick is and where it's likely to have come from—'

Paulo interrupted. 'What games have you got on your dive computer, Hex?' He wasn't joking; the dive computers had games to help them while away the time on the way up.

Hex pulled a face. 'They're really naff. I'm not going to look at them.'

'They're better than nothing,' protested Paulo.

'They're crude,' said Hex. 'I don't want to rot my brain with that rubbish. They're hardly *Half-Life*.'

'Well, it looks like you'll be counting fish for an hour,' said Amber. 'Try not to fall asleep.' She kneeled down and clipped their fins on while they did a final kit check. Then she settled back on a cushion with a good book and a sunhat.

Hex checked the video camera was fully charged. Then the boys moved from the central bench to the one around the edge of the boat. The boat sank alarmingly on that side: the kit was really heavy. Hex put his regulator in his mouth, then tipped over backwards into the water, followed by Paulo.

The sea out here was different from that in the shallows. There were fewer creatures, and the bottom was invisible, with the water below them dimming to black before they could see any signs of the sea bed. Paulo and Hex turned their torches on and headed down. It was eerie. Hex tried not to think about it but, being naturally claustrophobic, he felt as if he was being swallowed by a vast, cold blackness and he was very glad Paulo was with him.

A school of barracuda followed them in a menacing silver cloud. Paulo knew they were just attracted by the lights and wouldn't attack but it was still unnerving. One swam beside him, a long thin strip of silver with a grim face like a mouth carved into a rifle bullet.

They descended and left the barracuda behind. It was colder, a vast expanse of black. They kept checking their dive computers – to keep a sense of direction and to make sure the currents weren't taking them off course.

The bottom loomed up palely, like an area of fog, then became solid.

Paulo's torch beam caught a bubble of oil. He turned to Hex and pointed. They must be close. They could feel the current pushing against them. Another bubble went past. The current was definitely going north.

They would have to swim against it.

The bottom was bare rock like the surface of the moon, with no sign of a drill site. Hex checked his dive computer. They were slightly off course. They had drifted after all. He pointed with his torch. Paulo followed him.

The drill site loomed up like everything else, as a blur that gradually became solid. Something upright that didn't look like the moonscape elsewhere became a dull red metal pipe fifty centimetres long, sticking right up out of the sea floor. When they got up to it, they could see how big it was – a good two handspans wide. About five metres away was another, and after that another. It reminded Paulo of a plantation of trees. There must have been at least eight boreholes – and possibly more that they couldn't see. But one was clearly leaking – oil bubbling out into the sea like a black tongue.

There was debris scattered between the boreholes – more big lengths of pipe – as though someone had dismantled some scaffolding on the sea floor and just left it there. Hex filmed it: filmed the collar of cement that held the borehole in place, the dark oil swelling out of the top and breaking into bubbles. He filmed Paulo scooping the oil into Mara's sample tubes. Then he reached for Paulo's wrist and filmed the compass on his dive computer – that way they would have a grid reference to show exactly where the boreholes were.

Paulo looked at the borehole. How could it have been left like that? Surely there must be some sort of cap. He shone his torch in the top of the borehole and saw a big metal cap inside the pipe. It had been sealed, but not very well. He swam over to the next one. So had that. They all had. The oil that was coming onto the shore must be stuff released during the actual drilling and sampling and the residue left on this equipment. Although there was still some oil dribbling out where the seals were weak, the original leak had been plugged and the oil would soon stop coming ashore. To crash a tanker ArBonCo must have wanted to cover up what they'd been doing very badly. Maybe they didn't want anyone to know how much oil was there; how big an operation the drilling would be.

He looked at his dive computer again. One more minute and they had to ascend to their first decompression stop. Hex was swimming around the site, making sure he'd filmed all the evidence. The pictures would be astounding – the site was much bigger than they'd thought.

Hex looked at his dive computer too. Time to go up. He clicked off the video camera and hung it on his BCD. His computer gave him his first instruction: go up to thirty metres and stay there for six minutes. As Paulo signalled *Up*, Hex pushed away strongly from the bottom. But something pulled him back—

He dropped his torch. It swung from its cable, bouncing light around the dark water. Something had him. He didn't even know what part of his body had been caught, just that he couldn't move. His breathing rasped in his ears, bubbles streaming out of his regulator. He kicked furiously. His legs. It was like they were being held by some long-armed creature. In the dark all he could feel was this . . . thing. His hands flailed to catch his torch.

Paulo saw Hex's light jerk wildly. He powered towards him. Immediately comforted by Paulo's light, Hex stopped struggling and stayed still, but at first Paulo couldn't see what was wrong. There were the discarded pipes, but Hex wasn't touching them. Yet he clearly couldn't move. He tried to touch Hex's fins. And then he felt it. A nylon fishing net, no more visible than a cobweb in the water, tangled around the discarded pipes – and around Hex's legs. Fishing nets were the bane of divers' lives. They were hard to see, incredibly strong and took ages to untangle. This was how dolphins often died, trapped by tuna nets and held under until they drowned.

Paulo pulled a piece of the fishing net up so that Hex could see it. Hex nodded; he understood. Paulo unsheathed his knife and began to cut the net. He had to saw to and fro to get through the tough nylon, but even when he signalled to Hex to move his fins, Hex was still trapped. The fins had sharp edges and ridges on them, like ribs, with a metal clip to hold them on. Hex pulled his gloves off to get a better grip, leaned over, grabbed a handful of the netting and started cutting too. A sharp pain made him pull away, his hand throbbing and sharp as though he had closed it around a blade.

Paulo saw him recoil. Had Hex cut himself? That was the last thing they needed. He shone his torch on Hex's hand. He looked at the net and there, trapped in the nylon web, barely visible, were long ghostly filaments like see-through strings. What were they?

Hex was shaking his hand as if that would stop it hurting. It looked very painful. Paulo had to finish the cutting himself.

At last Hex was free and the two rose up gratefully, looking at the dive computers to check their depth. They were blinking. They had stayed at the bottom too long – about five minutes too long.

They wasted no time in swimming to the first decompression stop, thirty metres up. They found the anchor chain, a black slanted line in the water, and hung there, one arm wrapped around it.

Both their dive computers were blinking red warnings.

Hex wrote on his slate: *Down too long.*

Paulo nodded.

Hex showed Paulo his dive computer. It had recalculated their decompression time. That extra five minutes down translated into another fifteen minutes necessary to decompress. They had allowed more air for emergencies, but not that much. They would not be able to do the last ten minutes of decompression.

Paulo wrote on his slate: *Follow plan. Shorten last stop.*

Hex nodded. The lower stops were most important; shortening the last stop wasn't exactly a good idea, but it was the best they could do.

Paulo started to play the game on his dive computer. Hex looked around in the gloom. His display kept on blinking, telling him he didn't have enough air to decompress properly. He'd have to shut it up. He clicked to the game. Rubbish – just a 2D platformer. But while he was thinking about how bad it was, at least it shut out the immediate problem. They might be about to do themselves a lot of damage. And his hand was really painful.

It was getting cold. Hex clicked away faster, hoping the time would go more quickly. But he kept seeing an image in his mind – an image of a viper with a bubble in its eye . . .

A sharp bang reverberated off the headland and out to sea. Amber threw her book down and grabbed the binoculars.

In the distance was the tanker – the only place it could have come from. The tanker itself still looked much the same, but figures on the shore were running about in a panic. Obviously something had happened on board. She shuddered. Was that the explosion Greg had warned them about?

She opened a compartment and pulled out the charts. As the tanker was between them and the dive centre bay, she began to work out somewhere else they could land, so that they could then call Danny and get him to drive the boat back on a trailer.

Paulo was wishing they hadn't done their homework so well. They were at the last stop, ten metres below the surface, their air gauges nearly at empty – and they were about to cut short their decompression by ten minutes. Cold pages of clinical text swam before his eyes: nitrogen bubbles floating in his veins and arteries, attacking tiny blood vessels, then rupturing bigger vessels in the lungs, causing heart attacks and strokes.

Hex wrote on his slate and turned it so Paulo could see: *Medic centre. Decomp chamber. ASAP.*

Paulo nodded. He took a breath but got nothing. His tank was empty. He let go of the anchor cable and went up.

The two boys exploded onto the surface, gasping.

Amber lifted her head from her book and looked

at them. 'About time too.' But then she saw something she didn't like. When Hex and Paulo took their masks off, they put them on top of their heads instead of round their necks. Some people did that by mistake, but it was a move you were supposed to save for when you were in trouble and there was no way that Paulo or Hex would be that undisciplined.

Hex was the nearer. She pulled him into the boat first, then they both hauled Paulo in.

'We need decompression, fast,' Paulo gasped. 'How quickly can you get us to the medical centre?'

Amber yanked the anchor up into the boat, started the engine and wheeled it around in one smooth movement. She opened the throttle on full and pointed it towards land.

'What went wrong?' she said. 'I thought we calculated it thoroughly.'

'Hex got trapped,' said Paulo. He slipped off his BCD and the tanks clanged into the bottom of the boat. 'We spent longer at the bottom than we meant to.'

Hex pulled off the last of his dive kit. His fins

were ragged where Paulo's knife had cut him free.

Amber looked at the headland. She could see a red shape on the cliff overlooking the tanker. A fire engine. Her intention had been to go straight to the road that came down that cliff, but now it was blocked by emergency vehicles, she'd have to go elsewhere. To the next bay? No, she remembered, she couldn't – that bay was inaccessible by vehicle. She could do what she had planned – go to the next bay along and call Danny – but that would be no good either because it would be too far to drive from there to the medical centre. She would have to make for the beach where the tanker was.

Ahead was the yellow sorbent boom and its pink buoy. Amber grasped the tiller and swung the boat around the edge of the pink buoy.

Hex slumped down on the bench, his head in his hands, confusion in his eyes.

Paulo shook him. 'What's happened, *amigo*?'

The radio crackled and Amber grabbed it. '*Fathom Sprinter* receiving. Over.'

'*Fathom Sprinter*, this is the coastguard. You are in danger. There has been an explosion in the tanker and you are in a dangerous area. Please use a different beach to dock, repeat, use a different beach to dock.' The voice changed. 'Lynn, is that you? Over.'

'No, it's Amber. Is that Greg? Over.'

'Amber, you can't go to that beach. The tanker's unstable and there's oil all over the water. It could ignite. Over.'

Hex was trying to explain how he felt to Paulo. 'I tried to stand up and just felt dizzy.' His voice was dazed. He looked at his hands, watching the fingers open and close. Across his left hand was an angry red weal. He banged that hand against the boat as the boat hit a wave but he didn't seem to feel it. 'My hands are going numb,' he said slowly.

Listening, Amber went cold. Paulo was looking sleepy too. Numbness; drowsiness – both were symptoms of the bends.

'Amber?' said Greg on the radio again. 'Are you still there? Over.'

'Here, Greg,' she replied. Her voice was brisk. 'I've got two divers here with the bends. I don't have time for a detour; they're showing symptoms and they need decompression immediately. Over and out.'

Hex looked as though he was calm and floppy, but inside he was panicking. He felt trapped in a tingling, fuzzy body that didn't obey him any more. He couldn't even scratch where his skin felt itchy. He was perfectly aware of what was going on, but felt totally helpless.

Amber was alongside the tanker now. She could see the slope of its deck as it poked out of the water. Her heart pounded in her throat as she pushed the throttle further, but the engine was giving her its top speed. The *Fathom Sprinter* was making a deep wake in the water, pushing aside the oily scum on the surface. It was all flammable. Past the tanker now, just the home stretch to go, but still they were surrounded by oil. Ahead on the shore, firemen were waving to her frantically, the fluorescent stripes on their uniforms accentuating their agitation. 'Go back,' their signals were saying. 'Go back.'

She couldn't go back. Every second counted. She was less than 300 metres away from the shore now. Now 200 metres. Paulo and Hex looked as though they had gone to sleep. 'Not long, guys,' she called. Behind her the boat's engine churned the oily water into a coffee-coloured wake.

Suddenly she was surrounded by firemen wading into the water. She cut the engine. She'd done it.

'Those two,' she gasped, out of breath. 'They've got the bends.' A fireman grasped her around the waist and lifted her out. Behind her, more were lifting out the unresisting bodies of Hex and Paulo.

9

THE CHAMBER

The decompression chamber was a yellow cylinder four metres long and a metre wide – a solid metal capsule at one end of the room. Pipes and valves came out of its sides and connected to a big compressor that pumped pressurized air into the chamber.

It was split into two halves, each with a couple of hospital trolleys so that patients could lie down. In one half, through a tiny glass window, another patient wearing a transparent oxygen mask watched Hex and Paulo settle into the new compartment while their three friends stood around an intercom talking to them.

'Interesting outfits,' said Amber to the boys. They were wearing white cotton T-shirts and boxer shorts. Usually they were strictly men in black.

'Mara made us put them on,' said Paulo. His voice through the intercom was a little crackly.

'We're not allowed synthetic fibres in case they have to give us oxygen. They could catch fire.'

'Oh my,' said Li. 'Clothes catching fire.'

Paulo managed a seductive grin. 'This is a regular problem of mine.' But his eyes looked hollow and tired.

'So, no palmtop for you, Hex,' said Amber.

Hex gave her a withering look, slightly blurred by the thickness of the glass. 'The pressure would probably upset it anyway,' he said.

'Doh!' said Amber, smacking her forehead with the palm of her hand. 'How could I not know that?' But she was worried. Hex looked even worse than Paulo.

The chamber began to pressurize. There was a faint hiss, then a high-pitched whine like a jet engine powering up. Inside the chamber, the pressure was rising. Paulo and Hex were now 'diving'.

Mara had downloaded an entire record of the boys' dive from the wrist-mounted computers – depths, timings, the gases they had been breathing. She was closely watching a bank of dials, pressure meters and lights, although they were all controlled by her laptop. 'As we increase the pressure the bubbles should dissolve,' she explained. 'Then we gradually bring them to normal surface atmosphere. Of course it takes longer because they did it wrong the first time and we have to make sure the gases clear properly.'

Inside the chamber, Paulo and Hex started swallowing hard, looking uncomfortable.

Alex moved away from the intercom, his face concerned. 'Are they OK?'

Mara glanced in at the window. 'They're OK – they're descending quite fast and it makes your sinuses pop.'

'What about Hex's wound?' said Amber. 'On his hand.'

'A jellyfish sting,' replied Mara. 'But not a bad one. They're Cyanea – not poisonous, just uncomfortable. They get caught in fishing nets and leave tentacles behind when they break away. I see lots of fishermen with stings.'

Li gulped. 'Cyanea?' She spoke into the intercom. 'Hey, Hex, the jellyfish that stung you is two metres across and seventy metres long.'

'Don't believe you,' came Hex's voice faintly.

He sounded exhausted. Amber and Li exchanged worried looks. They both knew that Hex didn't like enclosed spaces.

The patient in the other half of the chamber was now lying down with his eyes closed. 'Mara, who's their room-mate?' Li asked.

'That's Andy,' said Mara. 'Don't take any diving tips from him. He dives too often. He's a dreadful example.' Her eyes were flicking from the dials to the laptop, checking that everything was going according to plan. 'He's also rather accident prone and managed to get himself shot with a harpoon gun this morning.'

Li and Amber looked into the chamber again. The patient had a big dressing on his left arm above the elbow. 'Shot with a harpoon gun?' Li repeated.

'Yes. The police have been here questioning him about it. He was barely conscious and didn't make a lot of sense so they're going to come back when he's more *compos mentis*.'

Hex and Paulo were now lying full length on their beds, looking even more like patients.

'We'd better let them rest,' said Amber.

Li nodded. She put her hand on the intercom switch to turn it off, but before she did so, she held up the video camera so that they could see it. 'You guys got some brilliant footage. The drill site's much bigger than we thought. We'll come back later.'

Hex propped himself up on his elbow. 'Make copies,' he called. Both girls nodded at him. He sank back and Li turned off the intercom.

'I can put a copy on my laptop,' said Mara. She put her hand out.

Alex was with Mara, watching the instruments. 'How long do they have to spend in there?'

'A few hours. Then I'll keep them in the centre tonight for observation and see how they are in the morning. But there'll be no more diving for a month.'

Li handed the video camera to Mara. 'A month!'

'It takes a while for gases to dissipate. Even you guys have got a few extra gases dissolved in your blood after that dive down to the tanker yesterday. Hex is particularly vulnerable – the dive computer shows that he was using air at twice the rate he would if he was swimming normally when he was down at his deepest, so he'll have more gases in his blood than Paulo. Quite a lot of the cases of decompression sickness I see are because something went wrong at the bottom, someone panicked, or had to struggle. They start breathing really fast – more gases get dissolved in the blood . . .' She shrugged. 'The main thing is, you got them here in time. If you'd had to get us to pick you up from another bay it might have meant a delay of another half hour.'

Li patted Amber on the shoulder quietly and Alex nodded.

Mara then connected the video camera to her laptop and brought up a program to copy it onto her hard drive.

'How's it going with the Clean Caribbean Consortium?' said Alex.

'An inspector's coming tomorrow,' said Mara, 'travelling down from Barbados. They want to come in person, particularly because it's a major company like ArBonCo. I'm also going to show them the medical notes of patients I've treated recently. I've been overrun by children with skin irritation and asthma, and lots of older people with respiratory problems.'

The video file finished copying. Mara pressed PLAY and the footage began to run.

Alex saw the dull red metal pipes like a tree plantation in the gloom. He'd seen it before on the monitor's tiny camera, but now he saw it on Mara's laptop screen he realized how big it was. He whistled softly. 'Well done, Hex and Paulo.'

Mara was horrified. 'This is huge. It's a major site. If this goes into production it will be a vast platform. There will be helicopters and boats going out there every few days and this coast will become like a bus terminus. The pollution will increase tenfold. It will kill the ecology and the dive schools will be gone for good.' She turned to Alex, Amber and Li. 'This footage really shows what we're up against.'

'Well, it had to be something big,' said Alex.

'Leave this to me,' said Mara. 'I'll guard it with my life. You go off to the festival now and celebrate.'

'Festival?' echoed Amber.

'There's a concert in the stadium at Willemstad. Reggae bands, jazz – you name it, they'll be there. Go on – let your hair down. You deserve a good time.'

Alex looked at the little windows in the decompression chamber. 'They do too. They worked really hard today.'

'Seriously, guys,' said Mara, 'you can't be in Curaçao at this time of year and miss the festival. I'll be keeping an eye on Hex and Paulo. You go and chill out, have a change of scene. You've done nothing but work since you came here.' She gave them her most severe look. 'Doctor's orders.'

Amber, Li and Alex would rather have stayed, but they got the distinct feeling that Mara wanted to be left in peace to do her job. 'We'll bring you popcorn,' said Amber as they headed out of the door.

Being in the decompression chamber, Hex decided, was like being in a space station. The room was cylindrical, the ceiling a mass of white-painted valves and pipes, dotted with red sprinkler nozzles. A slightly battered space station; the paintwork was scratched and the floor was marked with lines where the trolleys had been moved about. Now he was lying down, he felt better, probably because they were now effectively underwater again so their bubbles had dissolved. Funny. He would have thought a place like this would set off his claustrophobia but he was so relieved to be feeling normal that he was quite comfortable. Or maybe the fact that it was painted white inside made it seem bigger? He propped himself up on his elbow. Paulo was sitting cross-legged, inspecting a handle on the ceiling.

'The trouble with something like that,' he said, 'is that you're tempted to pull it to find out what it does.'

'Leave, boy!' said Hex sternly. His voice came out strangely flat.

Paulo looked at him oddly. 'Why are you using that funny voice?'

'I was just about to ask you the same thing. You sound like you've got a cold.'

'It's the pressure. It makes your voice like that.'

The voice came out of the intercom: Andy, in the other compartment. He had woken up and his gas mask was off. The intercom was above Paulo's trolley so he moved over to make room for Hex.

'I'm Paulo and this is Hex. What are you in for?'

'I got shot by a guy with a harpoon,' said Andy.

'I beg your pardon?'

Andy moved so that they could see the fleshy part of his upper arm. It was bandaged. 'I work at the aquarium. I was collecting specimens of fish – we're all diving like mad at the moment to preserve whatever we can so that we can repopulate later. On one site I saw a light – a guy swimming along. I thought it was someone I knew – another ichthyologist. I tried to catch up with him and he shot me with a harpoon gun.'

'A harpoon gun?' repeated Hex.

'That's a bit unfriendly,' said Paulo.

'Where was this?' asked Hex.

'San Juan Bay,' said Andy.

Paulo and Hex looked at each other. San Juan Bay was where the tanker was.

'Then what happened?' said Paulo.

'No idea. I was hyperventilating and panicking and doing all those things you shouldn't do if you have an emergency underwater. But it was such a shock. I had this harpoon stuck in my arm.' Andy was breathing hard as he relived the experience; no question that he was telling the truth.

'I bet it was a shock,' said Paulo. 'Did you see what your attacker was doing? Do you know why he did it?'

''Fraid not,' said Andy. 'I was bleeding into the water, and the first thing I thought about was sharks. That's when I got my act together. I surfaced as fast as possible and got back in my boat before I became some shark's dinner. When I got here with that harpoon sticking out of me, the police came and questioned me but I could hardly speak. I've been better since I got in here, but I doubt I'll be much use. One guy in dive gear looks very much like another. I can't really give a description.'

Paulo was certain there was more to know, but he had to remind himself that ordinary members of the public were not used to keeping their wits about them when someone attacked them.

Hex tried a different tactic. 'What time did this happen?' Andy should at least be able to answer that. All divers kept an eye on the time.

'About noon.'

'Why did they put you in here?' said Paulo.

Andy sighed. 'Bad diving practice catching up with me. I'd already done quite a lot of dives that morning. I've been pushing it recently – we all have, or the fish will be wiped out. I'd been down to about fifty metres already today and yesterday I did sixty and seventy metres. The San Juan Bay dive was one dive too many – and the harpoon attack . . .'

This didn't quite add up, Hex thought. His suspicions created scenarios at lightning speed. Could ArBonCo have noticed them and planted a spy to get information out of them? With all these environmental activists around, he wouldn't be surprised if they had. 'You were collecting fish from deep down? Don't they die if they come up to our pressure?'

'They don't die if you pierce the swim bladder,'

said Andy. 'That's a big air-filled space they use for buoyancy control. It doesn't hurt them.'

A surge of noise filled the chamber, like a roar of air. 'What's that?' said Paulo.

Andy shouted the answer. 'Air change. They do that every twenty minutes. Or we'd suffocate. Nice meeting you.' He moved away from the intercom and lay down on his bunk again.

Hex made sure the intercom was disconnected before he talked to Paulo. His face was serious. 'Noon. When was that explosion on the tanker?'

'About two this afternoon.'

Hex nodded. 'Have you been wondering why the tanker didn't blow sky high?'

Paulo nodded. 'If the chamber of oil and air had exploded there shouldn't have been anything left.'

'But there was some sort of explosion in there – what was it?'

Paulo thought about the circumstances. 'Andy saw someone – who obviously didn't want to be caught. Shortly afterwards, there's the explosion.'

'A bomb?' suggested Hex.

Paulo frowned. 'Why?'

'Because,' said Hex, 'someone doesn't want that tanker investigated.' He fixed Paulo with a grim look. 'We are not supposed to know what we know.'

'*Dios*,' breathed Paulo. 'At the moment we're one step ahead – but if they can do something like that, they're not far behind us. How much longer have we got in here?'

Mara had confiscated their watches when she had taken their underwear. 'I don't know,' growled Hex.

10

Showtime

Neil Hearst looked out of his window as the city wound down for the day. He had just printed out an e-mail on that day's progress on the clean-up. All positives – locals still co-operative, spill now contained and stabilized, beaches washed down, collection and removal of oil due to begin the next day. Hearst looked out at the sea. It was still a pure glittering blue, as if nothing had happened. Willemstad was quite a few miles up the coast from where the tanker had grounded and it was untouched.

Crashing the tanker had been a risky strategy, but

the leak from the drill site had nearly given away too much too soon. And now the damage had been contained. In a few years' time, once everyone had adjusted, few people would complain. Especially when the new wells were producing.

Tubular Bells. Hearst saw on the screen who was calling. He steeled himself. Although the tanker was out of sight, it seemed he wouldn't be able to put it out of his mind for long. 'Yes, Simon?'

'What happened to the bomb? He was supposed to put the bomb on board.'

'He did.'

'Well, why is the ship still there? I saw it on the news this evening and it's beginning to make my eyes hurt. What went wrong?'

'The bomb did go off. But it hardly did anything.'

'Why?'

Hearst's voice rose angrily. 'I don't know why. Maybe the powder got damp.'

'Don't take that tone with me. You told me the tanker was highly unstable. Likely to go up at any minute. But you can't seem to make it go off even by putting a *bomb* in it!'

'The diver must have put it in the wrong place,' said Hearst limply.

'Well, never mind about that now. You know we've got something far more important to worry about. You'd better not mess up tonight.'

Hearst's voice was flinty. 'We won't mess up, don't you worry.'

Normally used for cricket, the stadium in Willemstad had been converted into a massive auditorium. The pitch had been laid with a wooden floor to turn it into a huge dance area. At the scoreboard end was a large stage, surrounded by a stack of black speakers and tall poles with lighting rigs. The scoreboard itself had been covered with an enormous screen, which played a video from one of the event's sponsors, illuminating the shadowy items on the stage – a sprawling drum kit, spindly microphone stands, guitars propped upright, keyboards on slender black frames, the black wedges of sound monitors. A band's kit, ready for the performers.

Amber and Li moved purposefully down the steps

to ground level. Alex, Danny, Carl and Lynn followed.

'Do we really want to dance?' said Carl. 'I'm a scientist. I don't dance.'

'Yeah,' agreed Alex. 'I've got two left feet.'

Li turned and glared at them. 'Yes, we *do* want to dance.' She and Amber continued marching downwards, on a mission.

A murmur of excitement went up around the stadium. A row of people in white boiler suits were walking onto the stage, forming a line at the front. Some were wearing gas masks; others had black smears on their faces. Many carried placards: LIFE NOT OIL; STOP THIS BLACK DEATH; STOP THE KILLING; ECOLOGY IS OUR LIVES. They were immediately joined by men in black jeans and T-shirts, the word SECURITY printed across their backs.

'Could get nasty,' said Amber quietly to Li. The gas masks looked sinister. A flash made her look around. Behind them, Lynn was snapping away with a digital camera.

They turned back and watched the stage intently. One of the security men was talking to the ringleader. The protestor was nodding his head, the hose wobbling up and down, but his posture didn't look threatening.

Alex whispered to the two girls. 'I don't think this is going to get violent. They look like they want to co-operate.'

His instinct was right. The protestors leaned their placards up against the front of the stage and dispersed into the crowd. Danny hoisted Lynn onto his broad shoulders so she could snap the empty stage with the protest messages showing. The security guards began to remove the placards and a pair of burly men in suits appeared to inspect the stage. They moved stiffly, as though their jackets were tight.

There was something very familiar about that, thought Amber. She nudged her two friends. 'They're wearing body armour.'

'Must be some bigwigs here tonight,' said Li.

'I know that guy!' exclaimed Alex. 'The one on the left with the crewcut. He was in the Regiment with my dad.'

Li looked incredulous. 'What's the SAS doing here?'

'He's not in the Regiment any more,' said Alex. 'He left to do personal security, guarding VIPs.'

'I wonder who he's with,' said Amber. 'One of the bands?'

'Hey, Alex,' grinned Li, 'go and talk to him – get us a backstage pass.'

She was joking but Alex took her seriously. 'Li, the point of people like him is to keep people like you away.'

'Rats,' smiled Li. 'It was worth a try.'

Danny lowered Lynn to the ground. Once down, she pressed a speed dial key on her phone. 'Hi, Ray, I'm at the concert and I've got some pics of some protestors. I can e-mail them tonight.'

'I suppose a photographer is always on duty,' said Amber to Danny.

'It's her friend on the picture desk at the *Amigoe*.' The *Amigoe* was the daily newspaper for the whole of the Antilles group of islands. 'Lynn carries her camera everywhere. She's had quite a few scoops just by being in the right place at the right time.'

There was a thump from the speakers and a whine of feedback. The sound system was on. The screen that had been showing videos now began running through the logos of the event's sponsors. The bodyguards had left, satisfied that the protestors hadn't planted anything. Ten thousand people, gathered on the dance floor or in the tiered seating, now became quiet with anticipation and looked towards the stage. One or two shouted or whistled. The show was about to start.

One of the sponsor logos remained on the screen – the red flash of ArBonCo. It provoked a few jeers. Then a figure walked out of the shadows and onto the stage, stopping at the lead singer's microphone. His clothes didn't say 'rock 'n' roll' or 'reggae'; they said 'office' – he was in his sixties, with white hair. A caption on the screen behind him gave his name: Bill Bowman, President of ArBonCo Oil. Three security guards stood behind him, including the two men they had seen checking the stage.

The hush from the audience took on an intense quality, like a stare. Resentful murmurs started to flit through the crowd like a breeze through a forest.

'I bet his fan club isn't here tonight,' muttered Carl.

'I'm surprised he has the guts to show his face,' said Danny.

Bowman's voice boomed out through the microphone. 'Ladies and gentlemen. First let me say how devastated, personally, I am by the tragedy that struck us on Monday. Tonight's festival has been months in preparation, the event of the year, anticipated by thousands. It seems so cruel that when it finally comes we find ourselves in such a dreadful crisis. I do not underestimate the impact—'

The air erupted. There was a bright flash that drew everyone's attention. And a sound, which the crowd only identified afterwards as their ears began ringing – a rat-a-tat like a machine gun, followed by a whistling like a firework but much, much louder. Alex, Li and Amber were suddenly surrounded by a mass of pushing elbows, screaming mouths, frightened eyes.

Then they heard something else. Two unmistakable cracks.

Someone was shooting.

11

SHOOTER

Alpha Force's training took over. Amber grabbed Danny. Alex grabbed Carl. Li took Lynn. They pulled them to the ground.

Alex looked up at a row of heads. Everyone had taken cover. He made eye contact with one worried face, then another. Over their heads he could see the stage, where two bodyguards were hustling Bowman away, their bodies close to him, as if in a rugby scrum, protecting him. Another bodyguard lay on the ground. He'd taken the bullet intended for Bowman.

Far away, people were running. Suddenly there were more shots. Different this time, thought Alex. The security guards must be chasing the shooter.

There was a flash beside them. Lynn had lifted her camera above her head to take a picture. Li, Alex and Amber all had the same thought – they admired Lynn's dedication but a flashgun might startle jumpy bodyguards into shooting at them. Luckily Lynn couldn't take any more. Looking at the display, she cursed softly. Her battery was dead.

All this took only a few seconds. Then the crowd seemed to wake from their stunned state and the screaming started. People were scrambling to their feet, trying to run, kicking those who were still on the ground. Children were terrified, turning from one adult to the next for guidance, but the adults were panicking too.

A woman tried to run through Amber as though she wasn't there. Amber stood up and blocked her way. 'Get down!' she shouted. The woman stopped, shocked, then did as Amber said.

Li was trying to calm the people near her. 'Stay down. Keep still and you'll be safe. You are not the target, it's that guy who was on the stage.' Her voice was strong and certain. She reached out and tried to touch as many of them as possible, so they would feel she was speaking to them personally. One by one, people stopped trying to run. One by one, they dropped down.

Carl, Danny and Lynn were on the ground. They watched Alex calm a group near him. His voice was assured. 'Keep your head down and you'll be fine.' They were grateful that someone knew what to do.

Others near them took confidence. They kneeled or crouched, kept their heads low, held onto friends for reassurance. They calmed others near them, encouraged them to do the same. The message to stay still was travelling outwards from their little group like ripples in a lake.

Lynn suddenly realized how different it could have been. She held her camera up to get a picture of the huge dance floor with its hushed audience, then remembered she had run out of battery power. Pity; it would have made an excellent picture for the story – the heroes of the evening. If the three teenagers hadn't done what they had, the crowd could have panicked and people possibly been crushed to death. Li, Amber and Alex had quite possibly averted a disaster.

Paramedics rushed onto the stage with a stretcher and lifted the wounded bodyguard. Alex quickly looked at the other people near him. Hearing someone screaming in real pain might be enough to break the spell. But no, everyone was quiet. He relaxed. Imagine having to take a bullet as part of your job, he thought.

Amber had seen him too. 'Is that your dad's friend?'

'No,' said Alex. 'He's gone with Bowman.'

It looked like the security guards had gone out of the stadium in pursuit of the shooter. They were probably all safe to move now – but if this wasn't handled well, there might be another panic.

A voice came over the speakers. 'Ladies and gentlemen . . . this is the front of house manager. We . . .' The voice faltered as though he wasn't quite sure what to say next. 'We apologize for the interruption to tonight's programme. We will reschedule for a later date. The police are on their way and they have asked if you would remain in your seats as they will need statements. If you're on the dance-floor area would you please sit down. Do not try to leave the building. Thank you.'

A sound rose from the stadium as several thousand people shuffled and shifted, trying to get comfortable. They started to talk again – and to the three friends it felt like normality was returning. But on the floor of the stage where Bowman had been standing was a red, sticky pool: the bodyguard's blood.

Lynn had put another battery in her camera and was reviewing her pictures. One was particularly interesting – a shot of three security guards chasing a fourth man up the steps of the stands. 'Darn, it's blurred,' she sighed.

'I bet nobody else has got it,' said Danny, folding his long legs into a cross-legged position. 'You'll make the front page.' He looked nervously up at the exit in the picture. 'Let's just hope he doesn't come back.'

Alex was looking in that direction too. 'I think the shooter's long gone.'

* * *

'Well, thanks for an exciting evening,' said Li as Danny pulled up near the medical centre. 'We must go out with you guys again.' She slid open the door of the navy blue dive school people carrier and got out.

Amber and Alex followed her.

'Give our regards to Paulo and Hex,' said Danny.

'Thanks for the ride,' said Alex, sliding the door closed.

As Danny's tail lights dwindled away down the road they relaxed. Only now did they feel they could really talk about what had happened.

'I can't say I'm surprised someone took a shot at ArBonCo,' said Li.

'But an assassin?' queried Alex. 'This is getting a bit extreme.'

'People are upset,' said Amber. 'It's what they do. Wait till we tell the others.'

The night staff were on duty. As they pushed open the door, the nurse on reception recognized them and directed them to a room.

Hex and Paulo had finished their decompression treatment for the evening and had been moved to a private room. They were sitting cross-legged on the floor, still in their white T-shirts and boxer shorts, playing a card game.

Hex looked up. 'Hi,' he said, putting some cards down on the pile in front of him.

Paulo cursed quietly in Spanish and prepared to put his cards down in reply.

'Had a nice evening?' said Li.

'Mm,' said Hex, but he was more interested in watching Paulo. The big Argentinian was still thinking about his next move. Without looking up he asked, 'Did you catch the assassin?'

His remark took the wind right out of Amber's sails. 'How did you know what happened?'

'We were listening to the broadcast of the concert on the internet,' said Hex. 'Then I looked it up on Reuters.' He reached for his palmtop on the bed and handed it to Alex. It was a short report, with little detail.

Amber peered over Alex's shoulder as he read. 'Does it say what happened to Bowman?'

Alex finished reading and passed her the palmtop. 'Just that his security chief got him away.'

Amber skimmed the report. It didn't add much to what they already knew.

Alex sat down on the bed. 'It looked like a professional job. The explosions beforehand, designed to distract the crowd. Do you remember that whistling noise?'

Li and Amber hadn't thought about it, but now they remembered. 'Yes.'

'My dad calls them flash-bangs. They're really distinctive – the loud bangs, then a whistle. It's designed to disorientate you. While you're trying to work out what's happened, something else can be going on that you're not looking at.'

Li leaned over Paulo, plucked a card from his hand and put it down.

'Hey,' protested Paulo.

Hex stared at the card. 'You dirty rat. You had that all the time.' He threw down the rest of his hand.

Li ruffled Paulo's hair triumphantly.

'Thanks,' said Paulo, grinning up at her.

Li plonked herself down on the floor next to him. 'So he was a professional. But something doesn't add up. He missed.'

'He didn't miss,' said Alex. 'A bodyguard got in the way. And then he'd probably missed his chance. The chief of security was too good to let him get a second shot. The assassin was good too, though; he'd planned his escape route and he got away.'

'Would ecologists hire a professional killer?' said Hex.

Amber sat down and gathered the cards together. 'It doesn't have to be all of them. It only takes one.'

'This is turning dirty,' said Li. 'How bad can it get?'

'It's got bad already,' said Hex. 'We heard a few interesting things too from Andy, that guy in decompression.'

Amber, shuffling the cards, suddenly had a thought. 'Oh – are you guys stable?'

'Nice of you to remember to ask,' said Hex sardonically. 'Yeah, fine. All those frightening nasty sensations have gone. That chamber's magic.'

'That poor guy Andy's not in such good shape,' said Paulo. 'They had to put him in a wheelchair to take him back to his bed.'

The others were shocked. Had their friends come that close to serious damage?

'When are you out?' asked Alex.

'Tomorrow,' said Paulo. 'After another examination with Mistress Mara. Now, do you want to know what Andy told us or not?'

Alex, Li and Amber walked back to the dive school. It was a warm night, the air still. Occasionally the sound of a vehicle far away drifted towards them on a gentle breeze.

'A bomb,' said Li. 'Whoever planted it must have been out of their minds. It could have been an inferno.'

'Is is me or is the smell of oil less strong?' said Li.

Amber sniffed the air. 'Perhaps we're getting used to it.'

They took the path down to the beach and soon came to the big wooden jetty that belonged to the dive centre. The moon was high and they could see the *Fathom Sprinter* bobbing gently. The water looked normal in the moonlight; the blackened shore could have been a trick of the light. But as they got closer they saw the small mounds on the beach as the sea brought its constant tide of birds and fish.

'Hey, guys,' said Amber. 'What's that?'

There was an urgent note in her voice. She was pointing to a large object on the blackened beach below. A white hunk of something was lying in the surf, the sea washing in and over it, rolling it gently, then drawing out again. It was large, still – and ghostly white in the moonlight. Alex thought it looked like the tip of a rocket – cone-shaped and smooth – but as they got closer they saw it wasn't metal.

'It's flesh,' said Alex quietly.

Their footsteps crunched as they met the coral beach. They picked their way along carefully to avoid treading on the dead birds and fish. The sea washed in, covered the white object and moved it gently, then withdrew again. Now they could see a pointed head with a black dot of an eye. An open mouth with rows of teeth like shards of shattered glass. A pectoral fin.

'It's a shark,' said Li. 'A bit of a shark.'

Alex switched on the torch on the end of his mobile.

It wasn't even half the shark – just a head, a ragged piece of backbone and one pectoral fin. It must have been big; this part alone was nearly a metre long. The sea came up over their ankles and Amber stepped back as the ripped skeins of the shark's entrails floated towards her like tentacles. The sea retreated, taking dark swirls of blood into the oily water. Down the beach was a trail of mangled flesh as each wave washed more of the dead shark away.

Amber voiced what they were all thinking. 'What on earth did *that* to a shark?'

Alex played his torch over the corpse. 'This is fascinating.'

'You are disgusting,' said Amber.

'No, look. You can see its spine. It's made of cartilage, not bone. It looks like plastic. I'm going to take a picture.' There was a flash. Then he inspected the photo and thumbed away at the buttons.

Li peered over his shoulder. She pulled a face at Amber. 'He's sending it to the others.'

Amber rolled her eyes. 'A nice "get well" card.'

The sea came in and went out again.

Alex was looking at his picture, then at the shark carcass. There was something strange that showed up more clearly on the photo – a big black stain. And something else. He went in closer with the torch. Yes, it was there on the carcass; he just hadn't noticed it in the moonlight.

'Come and look at this.'

The girls looked at Alex. His face was less than twenty centimetres away from the corpse. They stayed firmly where they were.

'Must we?' said Li.

'There's a big black shadow inside its body cavity. It's really weird.'

Li folded her arms, determined not to move. 'It's probably eaten something containing ink. It might even be paint. Some of these sharks are real scavengers.'

Alex looked up. 'This doesn't look like something it's eaten. You've got to actually see it.'

Reluctantly Amber bent over the carcass.

'You have to get really close,' said Alex. He was practically sniffing the flesh.

Amber sighed and crouched down. 'If this is a

joke I'm going to rub your nose in it.' Alex moved back to give her room.

She'd expected it to smell bad, but it didn't – it was clean and fresh, like the sea. But she could see why Alex was curious. Embedded into the exposed interior of the skeleton were fragments of metal, twinkling against the glistening flesh. She touched one piece. It was sharp. Definitely metal.

'I know it's weird,' said Alex, 'but that looks like the debris from a bomb blast.'

Li came nearer and Amber moved aside so that she could get a good view. 'There were sharks like this in the tanker,' she said. 'One of them must have found the bomb.'

'That's why it didn't blow up the tanker,' said Amber softly. 'This shark swallowed it and swam away.'

12

ECO-WARRIORS

Paulo and Hex went into the examination room to wait for Mara. It was only seven-thirty in the morning but the clinic was already busy. A figure was waving from the porthole in the decompression chamber, trying to attract their attention.

'Andy's back in the chamber, back to work early,' said Hex. They went over to say hello.

'Did you hear about the drama last night?' asked Paulo.

Close up, Andy looked haggard. 'No, I was asleep.' He yawned, the extravagant, cavernous yawn of someone who would rather still be asleep. 'What happened?'

'The concert was cancelled. Someone tried to shoot the head of ArBonCo.'

Andy yawned again. 'Bill Bowman?'

Paulo nodded. 'Yes, I think that's what his name is.'

Andy looked confused. 'Someone tried to shoot Bill Bowman? Man, it doesn't make sense.'

'Why not?' said Paulo.

Andy yawned again. He shook his head. 'Man, it doesn't make sense,' he repeated. A bleeper went off. He reached for his oxygen mask and gave them a little wave. Time to go.

Mara pushed open the swing doors. They went over to the examination couch.

'Is Andy all right?' said Paulo. 'He seems rather confused.'

'I'm just about to check him.' Mara put down the files she was carrying and went over to the decompression chamber. She caught Andy's attention and made a gesture with her hand. Andy copied it and she nodded and made another gesture. Paulo and Hex recognized the moves – they were a sequence of tests for nerve damage that they'd done themselves the day before. They would take a few minutes to complete.

Hex turned away. 'Did you get that picture from Alex?' he asked Paulo.

'Yes. What was it?'

'Some part of his anatomy, I reckon,' said Hex. 'The resolution was terrible. I sent him a close-up of my big toe in return. And you'd never *believe* what I sent Amber!'

'I sent him the inside of my nose,' said Paulo with a laugh.

'Could have been worse,' said Hex.

Mara finished her tests and came back. 'Andy's suffering delayed shock. It's normal with cases like his. He'll be all right, given time.' She picked up a stethoscope from the desk. 'Now, who's first?'

She listened to their chests, checked their blood pressure, watched them wiggle their toes and fingers and did the co-ordination tests they'd just seen her do on Andy, then she picked up a device like a pizza cutter and ran it up and down their arms and legs to check for numbness.

'You guys seem fine,' she said at last. 'You were lucky. But remember, no diving for four weeks. You run a far higher risk of getting a bubble.' She went behind her desk and made some notes on her laptop.

Paulo rubbed his arm. The pizza-cutter wheel was like having ants run over your skin. 'Is it today the inspector's coming from Barbados?'

Mara sighed. 'They've had a change of plan, what with this assassin running around. It's a shame; I wanted them to see that video today.'

'E-mail it,' said Paulo.

'Isn't it a huge file?' Mara questioned.

Hex smiled. 'Give me five minutes.' He had his palmtop on his knee and had opened it and booted up in seconds. His fingers flew over the keys, the screen blinking and changing as he hopped around from website to website. Then he went to Mara's laptop. 'Where did you save the film?'

'On the c-drive.'

Hex called up the file and tapped in more instructions. A few more minutes of digital dexterity and he was finished. 'OK – it's on a secure website so all you have to do is send the address and they can stream it.'

Paulo asked, 'But could ArBonCo look at it?'

Hex's smile played at the corners of his mouth. 'They could. But luckily it was set up by a genius.'

'*Hombre*,' said Paulo, 'if Amber was here and you said that she'd put you in traction.'

The phone rang. Mara picked it up. 'Hello?' A pause while she listened. 'I don't have time to talk to a journalist.' Her voice took on a note of outrage. 'No. The shooting was nothing to do with ABC Guardians.'

Paulo looked at Hex. 'I think we're not wanted here,' he said quietly.

Hex nodded. They got up, waving silently at Mara as they left. She acknowledged them, then returned to her phone call. 'That's ridiculous. We don't condone violence. We would never, ever hire assassins. We are a peaceful organization. And you'll find the other environmental groups are too.'

'Hey,' said Amber, 'no wetsuits in the bar – house rules.'

Paulo and Hex looked nonplussed. With no other clothes at the medical centre, they'd had to put on their wetsuits to walk back. Amber was alone in her criticism, however; wetsuits or no wetsuits, Paulo and Hex were welcome to join the others, as they sat round a long table in the bar, having breakfast. Carl gave them high fives, Danny stood up and pulled out more chairs and Lynn passed them a jug of orange juice and a pot of coffee.

Danny sat down again. 'How was it, having the bends?'

Paulo poured some orange juice. 'Something I never want to repeat.'

Li handed him a copy of the daily paper. 'Look at this.'

The front page was devoted to the previous night's events. MURDER AT THE FESTIVAL, said the main headline, and underneath were directions to a number of smaller stories inside: '*ArBonCo chief was target – page 2*';'*Brave bodyguard loses his life – pages 2 and 3*'; '*Shooter took revenge for spill – page 4*'; '*Editorial comment – page 8*'; '*Letters – page 10*'. Paulo spread out the paper so that Hex could see it too.

'They used Lynn's photo,' said Danny.

Lynn got up. 'Yeah, that'll help pay some of the bills while we don't have any customers. When's the next cliff diving championship? The money might be useful.'

'September, in Rio,' said Danny. 'Oh – the compensation forms for the guest refunds arrived this morning. I put them on your desk.'

Lynn picked up her plate and mug. 'Yeah, I'm going to go and do them right now. See you later, guys,' she said as she left the room.

Li looked at her watch. It was eight o'clock. 'What time do the ArBonCo guys start on the beach?'

'Most days it's been about eight-thirty,' said Carl.

Li looked at the others. 'We'd better get cracking before they arrive.'

Hex, Paulo and Amber stepped lightly on board the *Fathom Sprinter*, which Carl and Danny had brought in close to the beach. Alex and Li had already manhandled on board a large object wrapped in a blue tarpaulin.

Hex noticed the smell. 'Phew, Alex, what *is* that?'

Alex pulled back the tarpaulin and the smell intensified. A sharp smell of the sea and fish. But that wasn't nearly as bad as the sight of what was inside the tarpaulin: the head and fin of a shark, torn apart as if by some ferocious force. The air shrieked as seagulls got wind of the carcass lying below.

Li got to work with the video camera. She filmed the head and then zoomed in on the blast marks like tiger stripes on the inside of the body cavity, the glint of shrapnel like embedded mirrors, the little trails of greyish flesh that were all that was left of its internal organs. From one angle she could see out through the mouth. The whole thing was glistening in the morning sun, the creases of the tarpaulin collecting pools of watery, oily blood. Although they could have filmed it the previous night with the underwater lights, it wouldn't have been as clear as it was in the morning sunlight.

Paulo realized what the mysterious picture had been. 'Alex, you're a rotten photographer. I was wondering for ages what that was.'

'*I'm* a rotten photographer?' exclaimed Alex. 'What have you guys been on? Hex sent me a picture of his toes, and I'm not even going to try and guess what that thing you sent was, Paulo.'

'It's those phone cameras,' said Li, sweeping carefully over the whole carcass. 'They don't have the resolution. They're fine for snaps but you can't do anything arty or abstract with them.'

'I think those two have gone soft in the head,' said Amber. 'Look what Hex sent me.' She passed her phone to Alex. There was a picture of a pink fluffy toy.

'It was in the cupboard in our room at the medical centre,' explained Hex. 'Someone must have left it there.'

'What you keep in your closet is your own business,' said Amber. 'No one else needs to know.'

Carl and Danny stood with their hands over their mouths and noses. The shark was really gross, yet these kids were laughing and joking as though they saw shocking things all the time. Above them, seagulls were wheeling in the air, waiting like vultures. 'Er – why are you filming this?' asked Carl.

'Li likes that sort of thing,' said Paulo. 'She's a weird girl.'

Li looked up from the camera and glared at him, then answered Carl's question. 'It's for Mara; I don't think she'd like us to take the actual shark over to her nice clean clinic.' She straightened up. She had finished.

'Let's give it to the birds,' said Paulo. He, Hex, Alex and Amber took one corner each of the tarpaulin and tipped the shark head over the edge. As soon as it hit the water the air was full of diving seagulls, shrieking and tearing at the flesh.

One by one, they stepped off the boat. 'The beach is looking a bit paler,' said Amber. 'It was a lot blacker than this before. All that washing must be working.' As she spoke, a red van was parking in the road; ArBonCo were arriving to work on the beach again.

'It's too little too late,' said Li as they climbed onto the veranda. 'When we found the shark there was nothing trying to eat it. Any other time it would have been surrounded by little crabs. Half the ecosystem has died.'

The man and woman whom Mara was escorting out of the medical centre waiting room as Alpha

Force arrived were not patients. They were too assured, too confident. And Mara looked fed up.

'Mara, we've got some more evidence for you,' said Li.

Mara showed them into her office. It was a mess. Her desk, normally tidy, was a mass of papers and her filing cabinets were all open.

'More journalists?' asked Paulo.

'I wouldn't get all this lot out for journalists,' said Mara. 'They were the police.'

'Police?' repeated Alex.

Mara sighed. 'They think ABC Guardians are involved in this shooting. They wanted a list of all the members; what I know about them, what I know about their friends. They even asked me what I was doing last night when the shooting started. Fortunately there are plenty of staff who can confirm that I was here, but the police have a way of looking at you that says they think you're lying. It's ridiculous. No activist would want to harm Bill Bowman.'

Paulo and Hex glanced at each other. That was what Andy had said. They'd thought he was delirious.

Amber thought it was just as strange as they did. 'This may sound an odd question, but why not? He's the head of the oil corporation – a corporation we think has been breaking all the rules—'

'Yes, but he's not like that. He's highly respected in ecology circles, passionate about consulting the locals, ploughing cash back into the economy, being fair, working with them for the good of everyone. And he's just been elected head of the Clean Caribbean Consortium. I voted for him on behalf of ABC Guardians. He's a one-off. There aren't many other people in the oil industry I'd trust like him.'

'But the police think otherwise,' said Amber.

Mara sighed. 'They're convinced I know who did it. They think all eco-activists are mad murderers.'

Alex asked, 'Is there anything we can do?'

Mara put her head in her hands. 'Clone me so that I can do two jobs at once. Or turn back time so that none of this ever happened. Let's see what you've got here.' She held out her hand for the video camera.

Li passed it over.

Mara began to look at the footage. Her expression became puzzled. 'What is this? Out-takes from *Jaws*?'

'You know Andy was attacked?' said Alex. 'He found someone putting a bomb in the tanker.'

Mara looked at him for a long moment. When she spoke, her voice was very quiet. 'A bomb . . . in the tanker?'

Her door opened. Four uniformed policemen walked into the room.

'Dr Mara Thomas?'

Mara was irritated. 'I've already made a statement to two of your colleagues. I've looked at the photofit. What more do you want?'

'Dr Mara Thomas?' repeated the sergeant. Something about his voice made them all go still.

'Yes,' said Mara quietly.

'Dr Mara Thomas, I am here to arrest you on suspicion of conspiracy to murder.'

13

Suspects

Out in the bay a boat was moored at the edge of the area enclosed by the sorbent booms; the skimmer boats were starting to remove the oil. The five friends were walking back to the dive centre, but they hardly noticed it. They were in a state of shock.

'This is unbelievable,' said Alex. 'Mara can't have had anything to do with the shooting.'

'The police obviously haven't got any other leads,' said Hex. 'They've got to go for the obvious.'

'Who hires assassins?' asked Li. 'It's got to be

someone who can afford to pay quite a lot. It does look like it's some sort of organization.'

'She looked so shocked,' said Amber.

Mara had co-operated and allowed the police officers to lead her away, but her expression had said it all. The crime she was accused of was disgusting, hideous. The confident campaigner who had made outspoken statements on national television and represented the entire Antilles islands at the Clean Caribbean Consortium had looked lost and frightened.

'How can they think a doctor would do something like that?' asked Li.

The others just shook their heads in disbelief.

'I think,' said Hex, 'that instead of clearing birds I'd better get busy.'

One hour later Hex was sitting cross-legged on his bed, his palmtop open. The others were outside with Carl, Lynn and Danny, removing the birds that had been washed up in the night. He didn't notice that Amber had come in until she was standing right in front of him, waving.

'Earth calling Hex.'

Hex's head snapped up. 'Why do you think Bowman was at the event?'

Amber sat down so she was on the same level as him. 'Because his company sponsored it.'

'ArBonCo wasn't the only sponsor, nor the most generous – the TV company gave a bigger donation. I figured there must have been some other reason why Bowman was going to make a speech.'

'There's the small matter of the oil slick,' said Amber. 'Apologizing to everyone and so on.'

Hex turned the palmtop screen round so that she could see it. 'This is Bowman's personal area on the ArBonCo computer system.'

Amber gasped. 'You haven't hacked into ArBonCo!'

'Mara's accused of conspiracy to murder,' Hex reminded her. 'Anything goes. Anyway, their security is atrocious. I just had to find one code and I was past the firewall. Now I can go anywhere I want and I look like the systems administrator doing maintenance.' He took the machine back and hit a few keys. 'Read this.'

Amber took the screen. 'It's a speech.' She began to read. '*Ladies and gentlemen . . . First may I say . . . blah blah blah . . .*'

'Carry on reading,' said Hex.

Amber's voice went down to a mutter as she skimmed the text. '*Blah blah* . . . Oh.' She started reading the text out loud. '*We believe there are substantial reserves of oil off the south-west tip of Curaçao, reserves that will bring great prosperity to this island. But we recognize that with that comes great disruption too – and so I am here to promise you today that there will not be a centimetre of drilling, not a drop of oil harvested until all the proper consultation is . . . blah blah blah . . . This oil is your resource, in your environment, and while we want to get it out we want to do so responsibly.*' Amber looked at Hex. 'But they had already started drilling.' She snorted. 'He's just a big fat cat liar. I hate them.'

'Yes, I thought that.' Hex took the palmtop and called up more files. 'But look at this.'

Amber read the new screen. 'Survey reports of the drill site. There you are. He's a lying rat.'

Hex shook his head. 'No, look at it. There's nothing about drilling. It's only geophysical imaging and seismic surveys. No drilling – you just sail a ship over slowly and fire sound waves at the sea bed. It does no more harm than radar. Remember? I looked it up before.'

Amber asked, 'Are you sure?'

'Now look at the file called "CCC draft". It's a bit rough but it's obviously meant for a secretary to format as a letter and send.'

Amber read the letter. 'It's asking them to start an environmental assessment into the impact of drilling.' She looked up. 'But he's the head of the CCC – why does he need to ask them anything?'

'He's the head but that doesn't mean he can do as he likes. And more than that – he obviously cares about the environment and wants the CCC to do its job. Remember what Mara said an oilfield of that size would do to Curaçao?'

Amber nodded. She read from the letter. '*There has been no drilling this close to Curaçao in the past and before we exploit this resource we must explore the environmental impact fully.*'

'I found something very interesting on Bowman's system too. He's got spyware.'

'What's that?'

'An invisible program that watches things you do and sends a record to someone. Usually you get them by accident from websites so that advertisers can find out what you're interested in. But this one is just sending copies of his e-mails to someone.'

'That could be the system administrator, or whatever you call it,' said Amber.

'No. They're going to someone else on the board. Just one person – Neil Hearst, his chief executive officer.'

'Neil Hearst,' repeated Amber. 'I've heard that name before.'

'He was on one of the press conferences, making syrupy apologies. That first night, when the other guests went home. I might also point out that *Hearst*'s system doesn't have spyware. In fact *his* e-mails are encrypted.'

'So Hearst is spying on Bowman?'

Hex nodded.

'I don't suppose a bit of encryption has kept you

out of Neil Hearst's files? And try not to be too smug when you tell me.' Amber thought Hex's expression looked as though he was about to unveil the crown jewels.

'Hearst, it seems, has been sending e-mails to a senior civil servant called Simon Ter Haar.'

Amber was getting weary. 'And? You're meant to be getting Mara out of trouble, not being Poirot.'

Hex raised a finger. 'Bear with me. Ter Haar is high up in the energy department here. They've been exchanging a lot of correspondence, and it's all secretive. Even though they've encrypted it, they're talking in code. They are hiding something. Most of the e-mails just say "Call me". One of them says, "Our adviser could help with this". Could be to do with hiring an assassin—?'

'Or it could be choosing wallpaper for the boardroom,' exclaimed Amber. 'That's hardly evidence.'

'It is when you look at the sequence of e-mails. Hearst had sent Ter Haar a section from Bowman's speech – the bit where he promises everyone an inquiry before drilling starts. They obviously didn't like that. That's when Ter Haar replied saying that their "adviser" could help. And think about what we've got so far. We're pretty certain the tanker was crashed deliberately to hide the drilling. Was it to hide the drilling from the public, or from *Bowman*, who wouldn't have authorized it in the first place? I think when Bowman was about to make that speech with all those promises they decided he had to be silenced. It wasn't ecologists who wanted him out of the way – it was his own people.'

Amber had to admit it made sense. She folded her arms crossly. 'The moment I came in you could have just said, "Bowman's a good guy, his CEO's been plotting with some geek in the government. Bowman was about to blow it all wide open so they tried to assassinate him and make it look like revenge for the oil spill."'

Hex looked at her simply. 'If I'd just come out with all that you wouldn't have believed me.'

There was a tap at the door. Paulo's curly head appeared, with Li and Alex close behind him. 'So here you are.' He saw the serious expressions on their faces. 'What's up?'

Amber looked at Hex. 'I'll tell them – you'll just make an epic out of it. Come in, guys.'

'. . . these guys in ArBonCo hired a gunman so he couldn't give the speech.' Amber looked at her four friends. 'Any questions?'

Three blank faces looked back at her.

Alex was propped against the headboard of his bed. 'How on earth do you know all that?'

Hex looked at Amber. His face said, *I told you so*.

Once again Hex went through the evidence, showing them the files on his palmtop and explaining each step.

Li bundled her long hair into a plait. 'This is really nasty.'

'But it adds up,' said Alex. 'A big company like that would have the resources to pay a professional assassin.'

'There's one thing I don't understand,' said Paulo. 'ArBonCo couldn't keep it secret for long. Once they'd set up a drilling platform they couldn't exactly hide it.'

'By then it would be too late,' explained Li. 'They'd pay the CCC fines and carry on. The only people they really need permission from is the government. That's why they needed the civil servant, who could push it through from the inside. Bowman would have stopped it all and spent years consulting and assessing the situation before they could get permission.'

'Of course,' said Hex, 'we can't take any of this to the police because it's been obtained illegally. Now we've got to find a way to prove it properly.'

'Bowman is still alive, isn't he?' said Alex. 'If someone wants him dead they'll probably try again, won't they? I wonder if he's gone back to work as normal.'

Li jumped up and flew out of the room. Before the others had time to look puzzled, she came back in with the newspaper and laid it out on Hex's bed. 'They say his bodyguards got him to safety. They don't say where he is now.'

'If we could find out where he is,' said Amber, 'we might be able to keep our eyes open for another attempt. We could save him *and* get proper evidence.'

Alex's face was screwed up in thought. 'I think I've got an idea.'

Alex sat on his bed, dialling the ArBonCo press office on his mobile; the others crowded together on Hex's bed on the other side of the room. With notepad in hand, Alex looked every inch the investigative reporter.

The phone was answered immediately by a brisk, male voice. 'Hello – press office.'

Alex launched into his prepared spiel. 'My name's Alex Craig. I'm writing a follow-up about the attempted shooting of your president last night and I was wondering if I could ask a few questions.'

'Which publication are you from?'

Alex had this prepared. 'I'm a freelance doing a piece for the *Financial Times* in London.' Using a British newspaper had been Amber's suggestion, in case the press office had already been bombarded with questions from US, South American and Caribbean papers.

'What's your angle?'

So far, so good. This was what they'd expected.

'I'm interested in him as a big personality in the oil world and was wondering if we could talk to him.'

'That's not possible.'

'Is he well?' asked Alex.

'He is well,' said the press officer.

'Was he hurt in the incident?'

'He wasn't hurt.'

This wasn't getting very far. Alex suddenly realized where he was going wrong; he was asking questions that could easily be answered with yes or no. He needed to phrase them so that they couldn't be dismissed so swiftly. He grasped at straws. How did big corporations work? Say something about money. 'What are you telling the investors and shareholders?'

'We haven't issued a statement. That's all I can say about it at the moment.'

Now that sounded deliberately obstructive. What could he ask that they couldn't evade? Inspiration struck. 'Does that mean he's no longer in charge?'

It was a daring move and he caught a glimpse of four pairs of astonished eyes.

But his question seemed to have the desired

response. 'He is in close contact with his advisers and other members of the board.'

Alex pounced. 'Does that include the CEO Neil Hearst?'

This was going well. From the bed, the others watched him. Alex's face had changed as he got into his role; it had become sharper, like a hardened newshound. Li suddenly got an urge to giggle. If the press officer knew he was talking to a teenager . . . She stuffed her knuckles in her mouth to stop herself from making any noise.

Alex had the bit between his teeth. 'So Mr Hearst is in charge at the moment?' A pause, then, 'But you said Mr Bowman is well and unhurt. Now you're saying he's been removed. Are you worried there might be another attempt on his life?'

Another pause. After a few moments Alex said, 'And his head of security is with him, is he?' Pause. 'Oh really? I see. Thanks very much for your time. Yes, it should be in the next edition. Bye.'

A click as he hung up.

Suddenly he was surrounded by hugging friends. Li and Paulo got him between them and squeezed him hard. 'Alex, you were fantastic,' grinned Paulo.

'Listen,' said Alex, his face deadly serious. 'This is really important. They're saying he's unwell because of the stress of the incident, so he's having medical treatment. They've taken him to a secret location as a precaution. And – get this – the head of security has gone back to the UK.'

'He's gone?' repeated Amber. 'At a time like this?'

'That's what the press officer said,' replied Alex. 'There's something really wrong there. That guy had the same bodyguard training as my dad. There's no way he'd leave at a time like this.'

'No way he'd leave – voluntarily,' pointed out Hex.

Li caught his drift. 'Do you think he's been got out of the way?'

Alex nodded. 'Definitely.'

'Should we go to the police?'

Hex's face was grave. 'We can't – we still haven't got anything we can use. And I bet they wouldn't be able to find Bowman if they went looking for him. Hearst's holding all the cards. He's in control of the company and Bowman's bodyguard is out of the way. He must be keeping Bowman alive for some reason – though I can't imagine why if he wanted him dead. But if we blow the whistle now Bowman may disappear for good and no one would ever know what really happened. There would be an investigation into the assassination attempt and with no other suspects Mara might spend months trying to prove she had nothing to do with it.'

'We need more actual evidence, somehow,' said Paulo.

There was a long silence. Finally Li spoke. 'Well, I'm out of ideas. Anyone feel inspired?'

Her four friends shook their heads silently. They felt as baffled as she did.

14

DOMESTIC CRISIS

From far off came a roar. 'Legs together!' Then a splash.

'Carl again, if I'm not mistaken,' said Li.

'Back to his old habits, by the sound of it,' added Amber.

Alpha Force were on their way to the library. They'd decided to do some more revision on dive tables. Perhaps if they stopped racking their brains about the current problems and thought about something else for a while, someone might come up with an idea. Already they felt better, now that they had a sense of purpose.

They could see all the way through the bar and out to the bay. Danny was on his perch by Stormy Point, drilling his pupil. Lynn was on the veranda, sitting at a table under a sun umbrella, surrounded by a mass of papers. She saw them pause to watch Carl and waved. 'Don't you guys go trying anything like that,' she called out. She held up a jug of iced coffee. 'Want some?'

A cold, refreshing drink to take to the study – the offer was greeted with enthusiasm.

Amber took charge. 'Five iced coffees it is.' She took hold of Hex's black T-shirt and pulled him along with her. 'Come on, Hex, you can help me bring them.'

Hex grabbed some glasses from behind the bar and when he caught Amber up, she was already chatting to Lynn. 'Did you hear about Mara?'

Lynn ran her hands through her blonde hair. 'Yeah. The world's gone mad and everyone's jumpy as hell. I've had my sister on the phone this morning. She runs a housekeeping company, providing staff for big houses. One of her clients has started hiring an armed guard, would you believe, and now the maids are scared stiff.'

Amber picked up the jug and began to pour. 'Who is this client? A rock star?'

'No. He's only a civil servant,' said Lynn. 'A rather rich one, but just a boring civil servant.'

A well-paid civil servant who'd suddenly acquired armed protection? The frosted jug wobbled in Amber's hand, the cubes of ice tinkled into the glasses. Every nerve was tingling. She looked at Hex. His eyebrows had shot up to his hairline.

Lynn put down her pen. 'What's the matter? Spit it out. I know that look when you sniff a breakthrough. I've worked with a lot of reporters, remember.'

Hex thought like lightning. He was used to being careful about how much people knew. But would it do any harm to share their suspicions with Lynn? Of course not. And it could ultimately help Mara, her friend. 'We think that a civil servant is somehow mixed up with all this assassination business,' he said.

'And this guy just got an armed guard,' Amber added. 'Rather suspicious.'

Lynn nodded. 'I see where you're coming from.'

'He's not called . . . Ter Haar, by any chance, is he?' Amber continued.

Lynn started and then nodded.

'He's the one we think might be involved,' Hex said softly, a smile of satisfaction crossing his lips at her confirmation. 'It would really help if we could get a look at the set-up there.' He didn't share his major suspicion – that Bowman was there. Lynn didn't need to know everything.

'I can tell you where it is,' she said. 'When Sarah and I go out together she points out all her clients' houses. Terribly indiscreet, but that's my sister.' She smiled. 'Especially as she knows I'm a nosy photographer at heart. But I'll give you a bit of advice.'

'Yes?' said Amber.

'If you want to snoop around any of these big places, it's got to be you or Li. These guys like African, West Indian or Filipino maids. A white face among the servants would stick out like a sore thumb.'

Amber nodded. 'Good tip. Thanks.'

Lynn got up and went into the bar. 'I'll show you where the house is. It's an old place – one of those colonial mansions. It's marked on the map.'

Amber picked up two glasses and followed her. Hex brought up the rear with the other three. Lynn took them through to the reception area, and pulled a map out from under the desk. She opened it out and traced her finger along one of the roads, looking for the house. 'Just one thing. I'll help you, you help me. Personally, I've always thought Simon Ter Haar was a bit of an odd fish. Now you think he's up to something. When you nab the bad boys, call me to take the photos. Deal?'

'Deal,' grinned Amber.

Lynn made a call to a friend and they hired five bicycles so they could approach the house quietly and inconspicuously. As they left the coast and pushed upwards, the landscape became scrubby and dusty. Cacti were everywhere – tall and straight like organ pipes, or slender and jointed. There were few trees – the trees that did grow there were thin and stunted, all blown to point south-west by the north-east trade wind that gave the island group one of their names – the Windward Islands. The houses were mostly single storey with red roofs, the straight cacti arranged around them to form solid spiny fences. Wild goats were everywhere, eating the cactus fences or charging into the little group and sending them swerving, and deer hopped away from them across the scrubby plain, white tails bobbing until they became dots.

Occasionally lines of bright-coloured washing were strung from cactus to cactus – just like you'd use trees in your garden in England, thought Alex. In the far distance, like a roof on the island, was a forest of dark green.

Amber, Paulo and Li were wearing their tracers – miniature transmitters contained in lockets and belt buckles. They were connected to a program on Hex's palmtop so he would be able to monitor where they were at all times. He and Alex were to stay in deep cover.

It was midday and the sun was high in the sky. They all wore hats to keep the worst of the sun off, and stopped frequently for water breaks. Cycling in this terrain was hard work. They were fit, but still they paced themselves carefully. Once they reached their destination, they had to be fully alert.

Now they were into the plantations. Tall stems of sugar cane towered two metres over them, the slender green leaves at the top waving like palm fronds. The cane closed in like a forest, with only a strip of sky visible, making them feel as though they had been miniaturized and were cycling on a path between two fields of long grass. Now and again they got glimpses back into the bay. There were two skimmer boats out there now, collecting the spilled oil; the slick was like a shadow on the sparkling blue.

They'd made a plan and decided Amber should go in first, with Li as back-up. As they only had two possible personnel they could use, they would keep Li back unless there was an emergency, or Amber found Bowman in the house. If she didn't find Bowman, Li might need to do the same thing in another location. Amber would text progress reports, following standard Alpha Force operating procedures. Meanwhile, while Hex and Alex monitored the tracers from deep cover, Li and Paulo would make a laying-up point nearby in case back-up was needed.

Alex stopped and consulted the map. 'Hey, guys,' he called. 'Here's where we stop. The house is just round the corner.'

A small path led into the plantation. They pulled the bikes off the road and stowed them among the tall stems. Amber strode off into the plantation, her rucksack swinging over her shoulder. 'Just gotta change. See you in a moment, guys.'

Hex powered up his palmtop and checked the tracers. He picked up the three tracers and zoomed in: two stayed together and one was a little way away. 'There's Amber stripping off,' said Paulo, pointing to the lone one. 'Are you sure you haven't got video contact?'

'I'm working on it,' said Hex.

Amber came back out. The sleek, sassy young woman had become a poor-looking young girl in cast-offs. Her lycra cycling shorts and tight T-shirt had been replaced by ill-fitting cut-off jeans that belonged to Hex, a shapeless bright blue T-shirt that belonged to Paulo and her oldest pair of trainers. Around her neck was a leather thong with a couple of shells – the locket was hidden.

'Good costume, Amber,' said Alex. 'You don't look like yourself at all.'

Paulo checked the contents of his backpack and slipped it onto his broad shoulders. He nodded to Li. 'Ready?'

Li nodded. 'Ready.'

Amber nodded. 'Ready.'

'Good luck,' said Alex.

They set off round the corner and were gone.

Hex and Alex concealed three of the bikes and then settled down by the road with their two and some bottles of water. That way, if anyone came past, they would see two cyclists having a rest after a hard ride.

The hill sloped away dramatically in front of Li, Paulo and Amber. An eighteenth-century house lay below, looking out towards the sea, surrounded by sugar-cane plantations like a small ranch. Its red-tiled roof stretched out in front of them. They stopped and silently took in the layout. The ground in front of it was asphalted to make a drive, then instead of a garden there was a terrace composed of square ponds that proceeded like giant mirrored steps down the hill. The water was strange colours – fuchsia, violet, rusty pink.

'What are those?' Li whispered in case the wind carried her voice.

'Disused salt pans,' replied Amber. 'Salt used to be a major export of these islands. They'd leave brine to evaporate in the sun and then get slaves to scrape the salt out.'

'Makes a change from sugar,' murmured Paulo. 'Why are they that colour?'

'Must be algae,' whispered Li. 'Aren't they amazing?' Then she gripped Paulo's arm and nodded at the house.

Down in the drive a figure was walking up from a parked Toyota 4x4. Over his shoulder on a sling was a rifle. He walked into the house.

'Well, there's a guy with hardware,' said Amber. 'I wonder if he's the only one?'

Paulo looked around. 'We've got good visibility.

We'll lay up here while you go in, Amber. Text every fifteen minutes, OK?'

Amber nodded. 'Every fifteen minutes.'

As Amber walked off towards the house, Paulo shrugged off his backpack and pulled out a couple of pieces of a lightweight camouflage net he had made earlier from a T-shirt, giving one piece to Li. They put them over their heads like veils. It wasn't convincing up close, but it would break up their outline so that they couldn't be seen from down below against the sugar cane. Paulo also had a brightly coloured T-shirt and some baggy denims of Alex's in his pack for Li to put on if she had to go and join Amber. He put the rucksack back on under the netting and they picked their way further along the bank until they were deep in the plantation. The sugar cane was tall, towering above them as though they were mice in long grass. They settled down, huddling together to distort their outline further.

They had a good view all around the house. Amber had now reached the drive that went around the back of the house. In her too-big clothes she looked very young and vulnerable.

15

Ter Haar

Amber stopped to get her bearings. In front of her was a white-painted veranda with a couple of pillars to frame the front door. She was about to stride in when she caught herself. Servants wouldn't go in through the front door. She followed the drive round to the back of the house, stooping her shoulders and slowing her walk, trying to erase her natural confidence. By the standards she was used to in America, the house was like a cottage, but to someone who had to earn her living doing domestic chores it would be an awesome sight.

She came to a big garage. It was open and she could see a pair of legs sticking out from under a cream-coloured Mercedes. Next to the garage was a terracotta red door, which she pushed open. The kitchen. The walls were also painted red, but the paintwork was peeling and scuffed and long overdue for another coat. It was also spotted with small white circles and Amber realized she was looking at a genuine piece of Dutch colonial history – the circles would have been painted by slaves, either so that they would look like eyes to scare ghosts away, or to make flies dizzy. Amber felt like she had stepped back in time.

In the middle of the kitchen was a long wooden table, bleached by years of scrubbing. On it lay a tray with a silver coffee pot, a cream jug and two bone china cups.

A man came into the kitchen – the same man they had seen outside. He still carried the gun over his shoulder as casually as a bag. He wore expensive jeans and a T-shirt that showed a well-muscled torso – the kind produced by a lot of weight training. His hair was greying at the temples and his face was deeply lined, but he looked dangerous and strong – and as if he was well paid for whatever he did. Was this the assassin?

He looked at Amber and his eyes asked: *What are you doing here?* Not in a threatening way; he wasn't aggressive if he didn't need to be, unlike an amateur. He was a professional.

Amber kept her voice in a whisper. If her accent sounded too different from the local one, this would disguise it. 'I'm looking for the housekeeper.'

The man lifted the lid on an earthenware bread bin and pulled out a roll. He tore off a bite and spoke through the mouthfuls. 'In there,' he said, gesturing with his head towards the door. Then he raised his voice. 'Mary?' He sounded as though he was shouting through cotton wool. Amber looked at the gun while she had the chance; it looked like a sniper rifle, only without the usual telescopic sight.

Mary came through the door. A plump middle-aged woman wearing a uniform of black dress and white lacy pinafore apron, she looked like a maid in a film.

'Thank goodness, at last. Did Sarah send you?'

Sarah; Lynn's sister. Amber nodded. The less she talked, the better.

'It's all right, he'll leave you alone,' said Mary, indicating the gunman.

That was good, thought Amber. Mary thought she was shocked and that's why she wasn't talking much.

'Come and get changed. Then you can take some coffee through to the lounge.'

Mary gave Amber a uniform like hers and Amber changed in a sort of wash house, where state-of-the-art Dyson washing machines stood against peeling spotted walls, and baskets of clean laundry lay folded beside an ironing board. She tucked the tracer locket inside her sports bra, tying the leather thong securely to a ring in the strap, then put her mobile in the top pocket of the black dress and bent down to check her reflection in the porthole of the washing machine. She frowned. Straightening up, she grabbed a freshly laundered pair of black Calvin Klein underpants from the pile of ironing, wrapped her mobile in them, then put it back in her pocket. That was better; now it didn't show. She rolled up her clothes and left them in a bundle.

Mary was waiting with a loaded tray. 'Down the corridor, through the hall and it's the first room you come to. Come back straight away because I'll need you to help prepare lunch.'

Amber hefted up the tray. It was heavy. The silver was old and everything was monogrammed – TH. Ter Haar. On the back of the swing door was a plan of the building. Amber glanced at it, trying to take in as much as possible. Mary's voice sounded behind her, irritated. 'Really, you can't miss it.' But Amber had seen enough. The ground floor was mainly open plan, but upstairs there were some bedrooms that might be worth investigating. She put her back to the swing door and went through.

It was as if she'd been teleported into a different house. She was in a modern hallway, big and white. White tiles covered the floor and a double doorway led to a sitting room. This was pale too: a deep carpet in a soft grey, cream sofas and a large glass coffee table; a brushed steel fireplace, pristine and sparkling and obviously never used, was on one wall; above it hung a Cézanne painting, the deep colours made more rich by the understated surroundings. It was a reproduction, of course – Amber had seen the real thing in a friend's collection in Boston. She stuck her tongue out at it, then reminded herself she was a submissive servant. The silly uniform and the relics of the colonial past were making her feel rebellious.

Another door at the far end of the room led to a study. She heard voices coming from it and moved quietly forwards to listen. Two cups – he must have someone in there. Bowman? Instead of putting the tray down on the glass table she balanced it on one arm like a waitress, knocked at the door and went in.

It was a dark, wood-panelled room. There were two men in there, on either side of a big oak desk. One of them, sitting on the side with the drawers, had a big fleshy face and meticulously neat hair. He looked at her with pale blue eyes that matched his shirt. Ter Haar, presumably. The man on the other side wasn't Bowman. He wore a lightweight suit and looked like he was visiting on business. Probably his financial manager – Amber recognized the logo of a private American bank on the papers spread across the desk.

Ter Haar waved at her, barely looking at her. 'We'll have it in the lounge,' he said curtly.

Amber backed out with the tray and the door swung shut behind her. Coming into the room from this angle she saw how long it was. Beyond the pale sofas was a dining area, with another fireplace and a long glass table. Well, it was clear Bowman wasn't there. She dumped the tray on the coffee table and went out into the hall. While Ter Haar was busy downstairs, she could have a look at the upper floor.

The staircase was grand, reminding Amber of *Gone with the Wind*, curling into a wide sweep at the bottom, but tiled like the hall. Ter Haar obviously liked clean, modern décor. She skipped up the stairs quietly, making her movements purposeful. If anyone saw her they would think she had been sent on an errand.

The landing was wide and square. Three white doors led off it on each side, all of them closed. She went for the first on the left. As a servant she didn't need to think of an excuse to be there – she just knocked and went in.

The room was a bedroom, and empty. There were

no signs of occupation – no shaving items in the bathroom or clothes in the wardrobe. Amber noticed the fluffy white towels as she went past the bathroom for the second time and grabbed one, shaking out the neat folds. It was as big as a bed sheet. She bundled it up in her arms so that it made a big pile. Now she had a way to hide her face if she needed to.

The next bedroom was much grander. The bed was a big four-poster antique, like something from a film about Henry VIII, and the curtains by the floor-length windows were of expensive white linen. It must be Ter Haar's room. Not much chance of Bowman being in here, she chuckled. She also noticed it was very much a man's room – no feminine items in the wardrobe and no potions and lotions in the bathroom. So Ter Haar lived alone. That meant he had no family he had to keep his secrets from.

She made her way out again. One other bedroom, she found, was occupied, with a simple overnight kit in the bathroom – razor, soap, toothbrush and toothpaste – and just a basic change of clothes and a small rucksack in the bedroom. Someone who travelled light, she thought. Probably the armed man's room. Thinking that there might be more clues in the rucksack, she opened it up, smiling to herself. What was she expecting – balaclava and pistol?

But there was *some*thing in there.

Amber lifted it out. A dive computer. She quickly put it back, gathered up her towel and got out of the room, choosing one of the others that she knew was empty and going in. Now she could think.

Bowman wasn't in the house. So why was the armed man still here? Because he'd had other jobs to do? The assassination? Had he also planted the bomb in the tanker? The dive computer suggested he might have. Although he could borrow all the rest of the kit, when it came to monitoring details that could affect his own survival, he wanted equipment that he knew he could trust. Possible hit man; expert diver, saboteur. Vicious enough to shoot someone with a harpoon gun. He had a formidable background. And the dive computer showed he took care to look after himself.

A professional.

She brought out her phone and unwrapped it.

12.30. Time for a progress report. As the room had a bathroom with a lock on the door, she went in there, shutting the door and locking herself in before texting. '*BB not in house.*' She pressed SEND.

What now? She could look around for outbuildings in case Bowman was being kept there, but that would surely not be as secure as the house. The bathroom window overlooked the terrace, with a view down to the sea. She could see no outbuildings – just the garage, which she'd already seen. Maybe her work here was done.

She picked up her rumpled towel and came out of the bathroom. The bedroom door handle was turning. Someone was coming in. Amber thought like lightning. She could have relied on her disguise, holding up the towel and ducking by, but she heard an accent that sent shivers up her spine like sparks. It was slightly Germanic – Ter Haar.

'Wait a minute, I'll go somewhere quiet.'

He was having a phone conversation he didn't want anyone else to hear.

She flattened herself on the soft carpet and rolled under the bed.

The door opened and a figure walked in. Amber could see pale linen trousers and Gucci shoes. She would probably have found herself polishing them if she'd hung around for much longer. The mattress dipped above her as he sat down.

'Fire away.'

Amber held her breath. Ter Haar remained quiet, listening to the other caller. The silence seemed so long. Was that all he was going to do? Just listen?

Then he spoke. 'It's twenty-five million dollars each.' A pause. 'Yes, straight to your personal bank account. But you've got to get Bowman to sign that document or the deal's off.' Another pause. 'And then make sure he can never interfere with us again. I think he'd better go over the side.'

Amber froze. That was crystal clear: they had Bowman, they wanted him to sign something and then they would kill him. Sweat began to run off her forehead. If a man could coolly talk about another man's death like that, she'd better make sure she wasn't caught.

Ter Haar rang off. He got up. The dip in the mattress rose.

Amber tried to flatten herself as much as possible into the carpet, the towel in front of her face. What if he turned back and saw her? Her ears followed his every footstep.

He went to the door and was gone.

Still under the bed, Amber wriggled her phone out. Her thumbs worked like lightning. *TH planning to kill BB. I'm on way out. B careful.* She pressed SEND, then wrapped the phone back up and put it away; it was definitely time to get out.

She wriggled out from under the bed and opened the door. Out on the landing nothing had changed – there was quiet, with just the gentle background sound of plates being stacked in the kitchen downstairs. The finance man must have stayed in the study while Ter Haar slipped away to take his phone call. Yet to Amber it now looked different. This was the house of a man who was ready to order somebody's death. She hoicked up her towel so that it concealed her face and started to walk down the stairs.

'You. Stop.'

Amber froze. It was Ter Haar. Had he seen her

come out of the bedroom? If he had, he would know that she could have heard him on the phone.

His footsteps sounded harsh on the tiled floor as he came down behind her. Amber turned round, looking up into his big, fleshy face.

'What were you doing in that room?' The accent sounded chilling and surgical; the pale eyes looked at her coldly.

Amber's mind raced. Should she say something? Should she remain silent? Better to look scared stiff. Then he might think she didn't speak English.

He grabbed her arm and shook it hard. He was shouting now. 'I won't ask you again – what were you doing?'

Amber couldn't answer. The moment he heard her speak he'd never believe she was a simple West Indian servant.

Ter Haar shook her again, frustrated. Panic flared in Amber's stomach. He was going to push her down the stairs. A scenario flashed through her mind – terrible tragedy, the new maid fell down and broke her neck. There must have been about twenty-five steps; if you threw someone down them you could hurt them badly. She got ready to curl up to minimize the damage. Instead Ter Haar kicked her on the leg to get her moving and forced her to march down the stairs.

'John?' he called.

The hit man came out of the lounge and looked up at Ter Haar and Amber. His craggy face showed no surprise. The rifle swung gently from his shoulder.

Ter Haar was looking down on Amber. He saw the bundle in her top pocket and snatched it out. The black pants fell away to reveal her mobile phone. He held it up to show the hit man. 'I caught her thieving.' His voice was incredulous.

Amber shivered. He knew it wasn't his phone.

'What do you want me to do?' said the hit man. 'You could call the police.' His accent was English and regional, but she couldn't place it. It wasn't like Hex's or Alex's.

Ter Haar shoved Amber forward. 'No, I think you should teach her a lesson.'

She stumbled down the last few stairs in front of him, sweat spreading across her back like a cold hand. If they looked at her phone closely, they'd find the message she'd just sent to the others. Why, oh why, hadn't she deleted it? At the foot of the stairs the hit man took her arm and Ter Haar let go, as though she was a baton in a relay race.

Ter Haar turned her phone on and the screen came up with the picture of the pink fluffy toy Hex had sent to her. She'd kept it as her start-up picture for the week. Ter Haar saw it and immediately lost interest. He dropped the phone on the floor where it clattered and bounced, the LCD screen cracking and the glowing pink blob vanishing. Broken. Now it wouldn't tell any tales.

That told Amber a number of things. Ter Haar wasn't used to this game – doing things where people might be spying on you. Someone professional would have checked the phone thoroughly, not discarded it. That made things a bit better for her. But it also told her he wasn't going to keep pretending she was just a simple thief. Here, Ter Haar and his hired muscle were a law unto themselves.

And that didn't look good at all.

16

Punishment

Ter Haar walked off towards the lounge, leaving Amber alone with the hit man. She doubted that his name was really John, but she knew that he was very, very dangerous.

The hit man moved her easily out onto the terrace at the front of the house. He did it as though manhandling people by force was the most natural thing in the world. Down below were the strangely coloured pools of the old salt pans.

Paulo and Li were still in position up in the woods. Would they be able to see? What would they do? And what did the hit man plan to do with her?

She walked slowly, awkwardly, to give her time to think of a plan. The hit man pushed her roughly. Amber still had the towel and held it up to her face, whimpering into it so that she looked completely cowed.

'Be quiet,' he said. He reached to take the towel away, Amber pulled back and he yanked it again. Amber seized her chance. She flipped around in a judo twist, using the man's momentum to throw him off balance, but he twisted out of it, grabbing Amber by the scruff of her neck and dragging her to the nearest pond. Her feet became tangled in the towel and her neck burned as his nails dug into her flesh. As they hit the gravel, her knees crunched. The water loomed up, mottled fuchsia and red like a sky at sunset. As if in slow motion she could see the reflection of her own dark, frightened face and wide eyes with the powerful figure behind. She smelled the stagnant water and saw the slimy algae fronds waving like rotten spinach.

Then her face was in the water.

She squeezed her mouth and eyelids together. The

brine seared her nose like acid and she prayed she could keep it out of her eyes. The hit man pulled her head up and she gasped in air. It tasted sweet. But not for long. Amber's head was forced down again, her mouth still open. Her lower lip, tongue and teeth shovelled up a heap of grit, slimy things tickled the roof of her mouth and the brine fired the back of her throat and made her gag. As her throat opened she sucked in more. It tasted disgusting, like putrid vegetables. Her eyes – she had to keep them shut.

He pulled her out and turned her head so that he could see her desperate face. Her eyes flew open and she spat, hard. Briny, slimy, gritty water blasted the hit man full in the face. He roared, his hands scrabbling at his eyes. Like an eel, Amber wriggled free.

She didn't look back; she just ran.

Li and Paulo had seen it all. Ter Haar's burly guard was on his feet, spluttering and rubbing his eyes. Amber's long legs pumped as she raced into the sugar-cane plantation. She was coughing, but the bottom half of her body just carried on running regardless. Li had already texted Alex and Hex when they saw Amber being brought outside. Now she texted them again: *Amber on the run. B careful tracing. Pursuer has gun.*

The burly man lifted his gun and fired after Amber. Li and Paulo jumped at the sound.

Then he gave chase.

Paulo grabbed Li. 'We'd better find more cover. We don't know if he'll end up coming over here.' He started squirming along the ground on his front, like a lizard climbing a wall, and Li followed. They batted aside the slender stalks of sugar cane with their arms, like swimmers doing breaststroke, while wildlife scooted away from them – lizards, rabbits with white tails, bug-eyed frogs, non-poisonous whipsnakes as long as Li's arm. The two friends kept down as flat as possible.

Behind them they heard more shots. They stopped, both holding their breath. Was there a scream? They couldn't see out of the plantation now – which probably meant they couldn't be seen either.

Li let out her breath. 'They're not coming this way. Should we go back? Set up a diversion?'

Paulo shook his head. 'We don't know where they've gone. We'd better get back to Hex and see where her tracer is.'

Li pulled out her compass and took a reading. 'Well, that way's north . . .'

Paulo picked up a stick from the dusty earth and drew a quick sketch. 'This is the house, which faced south-west. This is the road . . .'

Li consulted the compass again, then pointed to a spot on the map. 'We need to go this way.' She took out her phone and texted again: *L+P safe. Coming 2 U*.

Paulo said quietly, 'He must have been trying to drown her in the salt pan so that she'd have salt in her lungs. Then they could throw her in the sea.'

Li's voice fell to a whisper. 'I don't like leaving her.'

Paulo's brown eyes were intense. 'If he's still shooting, that means she's still running.'

Amber's lungs were bursting, her legs burning. Her mouth felt scoured and raw. With her arms she beat aside the whippy stalks of cane, crashing them aside as though hacking them down. The hit man was behind her, running hard, the crash of his pursuit filling her ears and fuelling her with adrenaline. A shot whistled past her ear. If she stopped he would have a captive target. A deer crashed into her, but she kept her legs going, determined not to fall. The deer pummelled her with its tiny hooves. Still she ran. While she ran he couldn't stop to take aim – all he could do was shoot wildly. She must not stop. Must not.

Amber was fit but running at top speed was exhausting her. Yet still the man kept up. He was like a machine.

Where could she go? What could she do? Where would it end? He had a gun. It could just come down to who was the fitter. Although he was stronger, Amber had age on her side; she must be a good twenty years younger. She'd have to exhaust him.

Her breath was deafening in her ears, her blood roaring like a hurricane, but she could still hear the breathing of her pursuer and the sound of his footfalls. That was more frightening than any hurricane.

She stumbled into open space and her feet met hard tarmac. A blare of horn and a screech of brakes – a long, dusty red bonnet, then the back end of a pick-up truck flashing past. Amber found even more adrenaline and pumped her legs faster, plunging into the plantation on the other side of the road. She heard the horn again and hoped to hear a thump, but nothing came. Still, even if the truck hadn't knocked the hit man over it would have given her a lead. She raced on. Now the ground was sloping downwards . . . and under her feet was short, close-cropped grass.

Suddenly in front of her – a cliff edge. Below was the sea, white waves thrashing on jagged rocks. Her arms windmilled madly, then she recovered her balance and staggered back. She had nearly gone over.

But he was still coming, crashing closer and closer. Could she get past him again and back into the plantation? No. He would be able to stop and then he could shoot her. He'd certainly get her.

There was nowhere else for her to go.

Amber looked into the water below. It was at least thirty metres down, more than the height Danny had dived in his championship – a competition in which his opponent had been seriously injured. What chance did she have? She pulled herself up sternly. No good panicking, she told herself. You've seen a lesson. *Focus*. She thought of Danny doing his champion dive; she would pretend she was him. She launched herself up.

But her feet hadn't left the ground. She was still standing on the edge of the cliff. A dead goat was slumped bonelessly on a ledge halfway down, its eye staring up. Her body wouldn't allow her to jump.

The sugar cane crunched and snapped behind her. The hit man was there, his face red. He skidded to his knees and she turned and looked down the black hole of his gun barrel. Even after running like that he was ready to fire.

Time stopped. She was in the air, aware not of falling but of the wind. She struggled to keep her body straight, as though she was a mummy bandaged to a board. When she hit the water, feet first with her toes pointed and her legs clamped as hard together as it was possible, it was hard, like hitting a pane of glass. It shook her teeth.

She burst to the surface, spluttering, inhaling seawater and shooting it out again. Her first thought was that, after the brine, it tasted positively sweet. Then she got a mouthful of oil and it was like licking an engine. The jagged rocks were a few metres away and she began to swim towards them, but the current was sweeping her away.

Already exhausted, Amber couldn't fight it. She saw the bulky figure up on the cliff she'd dived from; the hit man looking down like a vulture. The choppy water kept closing over her head like a counterpane. When she next surfaced she saw him turning away, as though he no longer had to check whether she was being pulled out to sea.

17

MAYDAY

Hex and Alex sat in the plantation monitoring the traces. Amber's blip raced through the plantation, paused – and went into the sea.

Alex grabbed his mobile and phoned the coastguard. 'I've just seen a woman go into the sea at—' Hex handed him the palmtop and Alex read off the co-ordinates. He finished the call. 'Greg's going to get her now.'

Hex nodded. 'Li and Paulo are quite close. They should be here in a few minutes.'

Alex stared at the screen with its three dots for a

moment. 'Can you tune into coastguard frequencies on that thing? We could listen to what's going on.'

Hex shook his head. 'It's not a radio, you berk.'

They settled down to wait for Li and Paulo, watching as they drew closer on the screen. Amber's trace was still there too, but it would continue working whether she was alive or not.

Alex asked, 'Will that thing still work underwater?'

Hex shook his head. 'Not if she goes more than fifty centimetres below the surface.'

They fell silent. That wasn't much help. Drowned people didn't always go under immediately.

'She's the strongest swimmer of all of us,' said Alex.

He meant it as a comfort, but it gave Hex a vivid mental picture – of Amber fighting for her life between the waves.

Amber was out in the wide sea. The land had become alarmingly small and all around her was vast blue. If she lost that scrap of white cliff she would be lost for sure. She had given up fighting the current and was just trying to keep her head out of the water, letting the sea carry her where it wanted, moving up and down with the gentle rhythm of the waves as if carried in a cradle. Her senses were drowning in salt – salt and the alien, metallic smell of oil. Her mouth was bitter and slimy. It was as if the sea was all around her, insistently trickling through every crevice and orifice, claiming her like a wrecked boat.

She became aware of another smell. Diesel fumes. Something hit her; something solid. It bounced off her and bobbed on the water. She looked at it angrily.

A lifebelt, bright orange. Drifting away from her. And beyond it, a diesel-belching silver dinghy.

She managed to find a shred of strength, kicking towards the lifebelt. When her hand touched its solid, smooth surface she had so little strength she couldn't get it over her head; she was just able to hang on with both hands. Then strong arms hauled her up, over the rope looped on the sides of the dinghy and into a space that wasn't wet, or moving, but dry and warmed by the sun.

On all fours, racked by coughs, she couldn't stop shivering. Someone put a red blanket over her and she pulled it around her tightly and coughed her heart out.

When the spasm subsided she saw a face she knew. He had thinning blond hair, a deep tan and a lifejacket printed with the word COASTGUARD. Danny's friend Greg. And there, at the helm, was Danny himself.

She managed a weak grin. 'Hi, Danny.'

Danny was looking at her in astonishment. 'Amber, how on earth did you get in this mess?'

Amber's sense of humour began to return. She considered saying that she'd just done her first cliff dive and that he wouldn't have to worry about her as competition for his world title, but she suddenly felt very sick. She clawed her way to the side not a moment too soon. Her stomach heaved and she vomited into the sea.

'Danny, slow down,' said Greg. 'She looks seasick.'

Amber glared at him. She was an experienced sailor; the last thing she would be was seasick. But as she tried to say something her body had other ideas. She coughed and retched, unable to speak.

'She might have swallowed some of that oil,' said Danny. 'We'd better get her to M—' He had been about to say 'Mara', but then remembered that she was still at the police station. 'I mean, the medical centre,' he said instead. He opened the throttle and the nose of the boat came up in the water as the propeller bit.

Amber leaned back feeling groggy and exhausted, her mind filled with images of the dead birds slowly poisoned by oil. I'll be all right if I get help quickly, she said to herself. Those birds never got any help. Another bout of retching seized her. The spasm was so strong she had to twist her hands into the ropes on the edge of the dinghy.

Suddenly the radio was squawking: 'Mayday – mayday – mayday. This is *Black Gold*, *Black Gold*, *Black Gold*.' A distress call; Amber knew the protocol well, the message repeated three times on VHF Channel 16 in the hope that someone was nearby.

Greg flew to the radio. 'This is the coastguard,

coastguard, coastguard – what's your position, position, position?'

The voice gave a position then suddenly went silent.

'Hello, *Black Gold*?' said Greg urgently. 'Come in, *Black Gold*?'

He was answered only by static.

He tried again.

Moments later the radio crackled into life again. 'Hello, coastguard? Over.'

Greg hit the button. 'Coastguard receiving, go ahead. Over.'

'Coastguard, let's go to Channel Twelve, I'm afraid that was a false alarm.'

Greg frowned and switched to the different channel. The voice came through again.

'Hello, coastguard. I'm very sorry about this. My son got hold of the radio. I'm very sorry and it won't happen again. Over.'

Greg replied. 'Understood. You're quite sure you're not in any danger? Over.'

'Quite sure. It was a mistake. I'm very sorry. Over.'

Greg spoke again. 'We're always happy to answer

emergencies but we'd appreciate it in future if you kept your son away from the equipment. You must tell him this is not a toy . . .'

Amber didn't hear the rest. She felt the queasiness return and had to lean over the side again. Her reflection in the choppy water reminded her of seeing herself in the salt pan. With the memory of its taste, she started vomiting once more.

Hex breathed a sigh of relief when he saw the small figure huddled miserably in a blanket in the dinghy. He left Alex, Li and Paulo standing on the veranda and skipped down to help Amber out as the boat rasped up onto the coral beach.

As he put out a hand to help her, she clung to it, quivering like an exhausted bird. His relief changed to worry. 'Are you OK?' he blurted.

She opened the red blanket. In her sunken, bloodshot eyes there was a twinkle. She was still wearing the uniform. Hex took in the short black dress with its white lacy pinafore, like a French maid's costume, now wet and clinging, grabbed the blanket and pulled it back around her.

'What have you been doing? You were supposed to be hunting for Bowman, not playing kinky games!'

Amber chuckled and allowed him to hurry her along to the others. It was as if he was trying to get away from this strangely dressed creature next to him. By the time they reached the others she felt miles better.

Paulo was looking at Amber with concern. 'We'd better get you to the medical centre,' he said.

Greg walked up behind them, a palm pilot in a rugged protective case in his hands. Behind him Danny was checking the boat over after the trip. 'Sorry, guys,' he said. 'Got to do some paperwork. I need some details about Amber.'

'Hex, you give them,' said Paulo. 'You know Amber best. I'll get her to the medical centre.'

Amber coughed as Paulo led her gently away. 'I reckon I look a bit rough.'

'No, you look lovely in that dress,' chuckled Paulo. Amber scowled at him and pulled the blanket tight around herself again.

'What do you need to know?' Hex asked Greg.

'Just statistics,' the coastguard replied. 'Every call

we get we have to log.' He handed Hex the palm pilot and a plastic stylus.

Hex zipped through the questions. It was all quite efficient – already there were details of how the call was logged, where the victim was, whether a boat was involved and what action was taken. One box asked if the cause of the accident was known. Hex had his suspicions but wrote 'no'. Once he was finished, he clicked 'done'.

The screen indicated there was another page to follow. He clicked on it, but the page wasn't about Amber but about a different incident. Greg had already filled in some details: 'Mayday call'. Hex was about to give the palm pilot back to Greg when something caught his eye. The palm pilot obviously had a link with a central computer because it had already logged the source of the call, identifying the vessel's position and registration – a big motor yacht called *Black Gold*.

Black Gold – another name for oil. Then Hex saw something that really made him take notice. He nudged Alex and Li, making them look too. They gasped.

The vessel was registered to Neil Hearst.

Danny and Greg were carrying the dinghy towards a trolley parked at the top of the beach. 'Hey, Danny, look at this,' said Alex casually. 'This is someone from ArBonCo. Poetic justice, eh?'

The two men paused as they went past Alex and peered at the screen.

A big grin spread across Danny's face. 'Oh yes, that twerp from the oil company. He keeps a yacht at the marina on the other side of the island.'

'Mayday call,' said Li. 'Has he sunk?'

'No,' replied Greg, 'it was a false alarm. He said his son had got hold of the radio.'

Danny grinned. 'You could fine Hearst for misuse of emergency resources.'

Greg and Danny heaved the dinghy up onto the trailer. 'Yes, we probably should,' said Greg.

'Do you need a hand with that boat?' said Li.

Danny went up to the terrace and unwound a hose. 'No thanks – we just need to wash it down, get the seawater off.'

Hex handed back the palm pilot back to Greg. 'Is there anything else you need?'

'No, that's fine,' said Greg, 'thanks.'

'Let's go and see how Amber's doing,' said Li.

They found Amber and Paulo in one of the treatment rooms in the clinic. Amber was sitting on a couch wearing the now-familiar cotton T-shirt and boxer shorts, her wet clothes in a bag beside her. She was sipping from a tall glass of black liquid. Hex watched her hand as she tilted the glass up, remembering how she had trembled when she tried to get out of the boat. But the glass didn't shake at all.

Amber saw him looking and held the glass out. 'Here, try some.'

Hex took a sip. It was disgusting. He spluttered and gave it back to her, one hand over his mouth.

'Well, what's it like?' said Amber. 'I can't taste a darn thing.'

'Coal,' said Hex, still trying to get rid of the taste.

'It's activated charcoal, apparently,' said Amber. 'To soak up any residual poison. Although it might as well be rose water for all I can tell. It's just a precaution, really. The doctor thinks I got rid of it all over the side of Danny's boat, otherwise I'd be a lot more ill.' She drank a bit more. 'Anyway, before all that happened I had quite a good trip. Bowman's not at Ter Haar's house. But they've definitely got him. They want him to sign something. Ter Haar and someone else – probably Neil Hearst, but I didn't hear that for sure – are going to get twenty-five million dollars each. Once they've got Bowman to sign they're going to kill him. I heard him say "Over the side", so I guess they've got him on a boat somewhere and are going to toss him overboard.'

Hex looked at Alex. 'Neil Hearst's yacht,' he said, then explained his reasoning to Amber and Paulo. 'Hearst has a yacht, normally moored on the other side of the island. It would be an ideal place to keep Bowman. Easy to guard and difficult to escape from.'

Li came back and handed Amber a tall glass, this time filled with bright yellow hydration liquid. 'So that's why nobody knows where he is.'

'Ah,' said Hex, 'but we do know where the yacht is now. It gave a mayday call. Only it wasn't in trouble – some little kid was larking about with the radio.'

Amber was glugging back the yellow potion. Her eyes grew enormous. She swallowed hard, then spoke. '*Black Gold!* Of course! I was in the dinghy when that call came through. I heard it. There's no way that wasn't genuine.'

Hex was playing scenarios in his head. 'Maybe Bowman got free and made a mayday call before they caught him again.'

Alex's face was grave. 'He probably won't have long before they get him to sign that document. 'Then . . .' He mimed a knife being drawn across his throat.

The door opened. Mara's colleague came in, holding a chart, and came over to Amber, one hand in the pocket of her white coat. 'How are you feeling?' Her accent was Australian.

'OK.'

'No more nausea?'

Amber waggled her hand to indicate so-so.

The doctor pinched the skin on Amber's arm and watched it, then nodded. 'You're hydrating well. I don't think you're poisoned but your stomach is very irritated, so you'll keep feeling sick. You can go, but carry on drinking the hydration solution – reception will give you some more on the way out.'

Amber's face lit up. Freedom again. Now they could get back to work.

The doctor was looking at her chart. 'You're staying at the dive centre, aren't you?'

Amber nodded.

'No diving for a week. Being sick in a regulator can seriously damage your health.'

Paulo looked at Amber sympathetically. 'Join the club.'

Hex was in the dive centre library. A map of the island and its surrounding waters was spread on the big central table; his palmtop lay beside him, open and the screen glowing. He did some calculations, then drew a circle with some compasses on a pad of tracing paper and laid it over the map. He looked at it, satisfied. That was it.

Amber and Paulo came in, Amber sipping at a glass of the yellow hydration mixture. Paulo was carrying a tray of sandwiches; he put them down on the big table.

Alex and Li joined them just as Paulo was starting his second sandwich and Amber was gingerly nibbling at her first.

'Danny's given us free rein with all his gear,' said Alex. 'So, have we found the boat?'

Hex indicated the diagram with a flourish. 'Here it is.'

The others huddled round eagerly and looked. Hex's tracing paper circle covered a large area at least as long as the island of Curaçao and its neighbour, Bonaire – which together had a diameter of about forty-eight kilometres.

Paulo looked at it. 'They're there somewhere? That's a huge area. We can't search that in time.'

'How did you calculate this?' said Amber. 'Did you get a zero wrong?'

Hex had anticipated their comments. 'I memorized the grid reference where the mayday call was made. Here.' He pointed to a spot not far off the coast of Curaçao. 'But they won't be there now because they'll know the mayday call will have given away their position. So – it's been ninety minutes, and I reckon a boat like that has a maximum speed of thirty-two kph and a cruising speed of twenty-eight kph, so they'll be somewhere in this circle.'

'But it's too big,' said Alex.

Hex held a finger up. 'I haven't finished yet. There's a strong current, so that means if they go with the current it looks more like *this*.' He made the circle into an oval.

'That's even bigger,' said Li.

'Ah, but here's how we make it smaller,' said Hex. 'They won't be heading inland, so we can discount this area–' He shaded an area around Curaçao on the map. 'They won't be going towards Bonaire either, so we can discount that too.' He shaded another area. 'And here and here are international shipping lanes, so they'll be keeping away from those too.' He shaded more areas on the map. 'Which leaves us with . . .' He spread his hands like a magician presenting the climax of a trick. There were two main areas left, one small and one bigger – about twelve kilometres across. 'It's an educated guess but I've been through it all twice and it came out the same both times,' said Hex. 'If I was them, I'd go here somewhere.' He put his finger down decisively in the larger unshaded area.

Slowly, the others nodded.

'Sounds cool to me,' said Paulo.

Alex reached for a sandwich. 'We know what equipment we've got and we know where we're going. Let's make plans.'

18

Black Gold

Hooded and masked, Li and Alex sped down into the water. On the surface, the *Fathom Sprinter* quickly became just a shadow in the distance. They were each holding onto a battery-operated sea scooter, a chunky propeller on handlebars capable of nearly 5 kph for an hour and a half. That was more than twice as fast as they could swim at top speed – but without the effort. Not only would it get them to their destination faster, it would save them air.

They streaked through the water, fins flowing like

graceful fish, without even leaving bubbles. Instead of normal scuba gear Danny had given them closed rebreathers – sealed units that took the air they breathed out, removed the carbon dioxide and topped up the oxygen and other gases so that they could breathe it again. This meant that they could approach the yacht invisibly, without leaving a trail of bubbles to arouse suspicion. Additionally they had covered their wetsuit hoods in a blue version of disruption-pattern camouflage – made from a T-shirt.

They both kept a careful eye on the compasses on their dive computers, but they couldn't help delighting in being able to zip through the water so fast. Shoals of fish hanging like clouds below them went by in a flash. If normal dive-swimming was like taking a pleasant car trip through the water, this was like taking a bullet train. And because they weren't leaving bubbles, the wildlife wasn't scared away.

Alex had reservations about the rebreather. Although he knew it was quiet to the outside world, the sound of his breathing seemed deafening as it was all enclosed. If his mouthpiece fell out in the water, he couldn't put it back in because the substance in it that purified the air became poisonous when wet. So he and Li also carried tiny scuba tanks with about ten minutes' air supply, just in case. But there was no doubt the rebreather was the right kit for the job – it was silent, their supply would last much longer and they would be breathing less nitrogen. If they did have to go deep it would not be so risky.

In front of him, Li powered her scooter down to half speed. Alex did the same. They both checked their watches: twenty minutes had passed. By Hex's calculations they were in the zone where the yacht was likely to be. They were ten metres down; now they headed up two metres so that they could see the brilliant blue surface more easily. Everywhere were shades of blue – inky blue below, bright blue above, and blank, featureless blue all around. Alex got a sudden sense of panic. He had been in isolated places before but here he was in the most isolated place of all – the open ocean. He shook himself. No time for panic; they had to search. He turned on his back so that he was facing the surface.

Li seemed to feel the isolation too. She stuck close to him as they moved along slowly now, both on their backs so they could see what was above.

A huge jellyfish pulsed past them, opening and closing like a gigantic sun umbrella. Li had never seen such a big one. It wouldn't attack them; jellyfish just waited for prey to blunder into their tentacles, and long filaments trailed from its body, curling and drifting like a stream of vermicelli, spotted with rags of algae. In the sunlight from above it looked beautiful, like an organic comet with an endless tail.

Li suddenly saw the tail swish towards them. They were drifting into a current and in moments they could be entangled in the stinging cells. She clanged her torch on the metal box of her rebreather. Alex looked around in alarm and Li pointed. *Dive!* They flipped over, gunned their sea scooters and swooped downwards. The jellyfish swam over them, its tail floating out sideways.

Alex and Li slowed. The danger had passed. Alex flipped over on his back again, but Li simply pointed: in the empty water a shape was hanging, turning slowly in the current. It wasn't possible to tell exactly how big it was because the water gave no perspective. But it wasn't a shoal of fish. Was it another jellyfish? No, it didn't seem to be moving on its own – and it looked too solid.

They approached slowly, keeping their scooters idling in case they set up a current that drove the thing away. It drifted slowly, as if suspended from a mobile. At any moment they expected it to wake and flash off into the distance, but it didn't.

Then Alex began to get a bad feeling. It looked human.

Almost. But there was something odd where the head should be.

Li looked back at Alex, her dark eyes uncertain. They cut the scooter engines and drifted forwards.

A body, hanging in the water. A man's body with his head obscured behind a cloud. Li clutched Alex's arm. Blood.

Well-muscled, nearly two metres tall, the man was barefoot, dressed in a shirt, casual trousers and a diver's weight belt. That explained why he was this far down in the water instead of floating on the surface. The cloud around the head made it impossible to tell his age.

The same questions went through the two friends' minds. Were they too late? Had Bowman already been executed?

Alex waved his hand through the dark cloud, trying to clear it. A face loomed out of the gloomy water, leaking blood from an ugly wound in the cheek. The man had been shot. Probably executed.

Alex made himself look at the face.

And recognized it.

Not Bowman. It was the man his father had known from the Regiment. He scribbled a message on his slate for Li. *Security chief. Not BB.*

Li nodded.

The body rotated as though it was on a string. The two friends caught a glimpse of the back of the head, a big hole in the close-cropped hair, before the black cloud of blood masked it again. An exit wound. Alex analysed what he was seeing. It wasn't a professional job: most professionals aimed straight between the eyes; this was below the cheek. Professionals also tended to fire a second shot into the heart. But professional or not, it was effective. And it meant that at least one person on that boat had a gun.

Li wrote on her slate: *Recent. Not eaten. Boat close.*

Something moved at the edge of Li's vision. Her head whipped round and she saw a big white shape like a torpedo. The sea life had just got wind of the blood.

Alex saw her slate drop from her hand and swing on its lanyard. She gunned her scooter. Alex didn't hang around either. They streaked off through the water at full speed. As Alex glanced behind, he saw a shark cannon into the cloud of blood at the bodyguard's head. The cloud spread like smoke from a bonfire, as though to mask what went on next. He didn't want to see it anyway.

Li slowed and flipped over so that she was again travelling upside down, scanning the surface.

As their heart rates returned to normal, Alex felt a wave of cold anger. He remembered how the bodyguard had once come round to buy a bicycle that Alex had grown out of. It had been a very small bike and it had looked comical as the tall soldier had wheeled it away down the pavement. Alex remembered his name too – Ian Davidson. He had just been an ordinary guy with kids. And these greedy crooks had killed him.

Li stopped and pointed upwards.

There was a big black shape on the water – about fifty metres long. The right size for a big, expensive yacht.

They looked for the stern, then rose slowly until they were just below the surface. The propeller hung just above them, ticking over gently. The rudder, like a giant paddle under the boat, was turned hard to the left to keep the boat going in a wide circle for a few hours because out here the water was too deep for an anchor. Here was where the rebreathers – and the camouflage – came into their own, because they were very unlikely to be seen if anyone was on deck. There was a boarding platform jutting out like a shelf above the water line. An entry point. Some letters were visible, distorted to jumpy wiggles by the rippling water. Alex went as close to the surface as he dared and the letters became a name.

Black Gold.

They swam under the platform. It was about fifty centimetres above the water line, so they were able to surface. Alex unclipped two magnets from his BCD and fixed them a metre apart to the underside of the platform. The magnets had holes in the centre, like doughnuts, and were connected by a piece of nylon washing line a metre long. Alex pulled it taut.

While he was doing that, Li slipped off her BCD and rebreather. Alex then fastened them onto the washing line, taking care not to let the mouthpiece dip into the water. The plan was for Li to go aboard while Alex stayed below until she signalled, but if anything went wrong, she could jump in and recover her kit.

They'd rehearsed this routine before setting off, and now they ticked off the stages: rebreather off, rebreather stowed, mouthpiece protected. The next stage was for Li to stow her hood and mask. Underneath the hood her long hair had been piled on top of her head so that it hadn't got wet, which could arouse suspicion. She could feel Alex under the water at her feet, releasing the clips on her fins.

He brought them up and hung them next to the other gear. Water slapped against the white hull as they worked and they could feel the thrum of the generator like a steady heartbeat deep in the boat. Li tucked her locket with its tracer – and a second tracer disc – securely down into her wetsuit, then unbuckled a rucksack from Alex's back and put it on. Ninety seconds after surfacing, she was ready.

Alex subsided into the water. As he went down, Li grasped the boarding platform and pulled herself up, her feet looking tiny without the fins. Then she was out of sight.

Alex stopped three metres below the surface. Here was where the wait began.

19

IN THE LION'S DEN

On the *Fathom Sprinter*, Hex sat up. 'I've got Li's trace. That means she's surfaced and is on the boat.'

'Good call, Hex,' said Paulo. 'You were right about where it was.'

Amber would have said something but her stomach was going through an uneasy patch. She sipped slowly at her umpteenth glass of rehydration mixture and tried her best to keep it down.

The atmosphere on the *Fathom Sprinter* had been tense ever since they'd watched Li and Alex plunge into the water and vanish below the surface. For a while the trace program on Hex's palmtop had shown only a blank screen. Now Li's trace had appeared, they breathed a little easier.

Amber put down her drink and leaned over the side. Hex winced. At any moment he expected the telltale sounds of retching. But Amber just stayed there quietly, looking at the sea.

'How are you doing?' Paulo asked her.

'Try not to be sick in the sea,' said Hex. 'It might attract sharks.'

Amber's voice came back sounding as though she was keeping her lips pressed together. 'Come here and I'll use your pockets, then.'

'Guess you won't be wanting a ride on one of these jet skis, then,' said Paulo, with a wicked grin.

On the back of the *Sprinter* they had two three-seater jet skis. Alex and Li seemed to have begged every favour possible from Danny. The thought of a jet ski bouncing through the waves made Amber grip the side of the boat hard.

Hex noticed and looked at Paulo, worried. 'Perhaps she shouldn't have come.'

'Yes I should,' growled a voice from the side of the boat. 'You keep watching that screen.'

Li crouched on the dive platform and unpacked the rucksack. Inside was an oilskin bag to keep the contents dry. She took out the black dress from the maid's outfit and put it on. The label said that it came from a big catering supplies company in Willemstad so it was probably the kind of thing worn by domestic staff generally. Her wetsuit was short-sleeved and cut off above the knees – the dress covered it nicely. The disguise that had worked for Amber should work for her too. She finished the outfit with a pair of black slip-on shoes and let her hair down so it hung loose. Lastly, she checked that she had the tracers around her neck.

She looked for the way up. There were three single-seater jet skis, a folded launch crane and— Ah. A white ladder.

She climbed the ladder and found herself on a big sun deck, with a wooden table and six white canvas chairs. Looking up, Li could see there was another deck above, with a large fringed umbrella visible. On the table in front of her was a chrome tray with three tall glasses containing a variety of half-finished concoctions – tomato juice, orange juice, mineral water. Li sloshed them all together into two glasses so that they looked like they were freshly made, then lifted the tray and set off. Now if anyone ran into her she would look as though she was fetching an order.

Directly ahead was a pair of double glass doors. She pushed them open with her backside. Inside was a saloon, air-conditioned and cool, decorated with honey-coloured wood panelling, white sheepskin rugs and a purple horseshoe-shaped sofa unit by a round table, where a man sat playing Patience. A harpoon gun lay beside him on the purple upholstery; a pistol was tucked into a holster over his shoulder. Was this the man who had executed the security chief?

The man looked up for a moment. His eyes crinkled as he saw Li and he gave her a smile that revealed bad teeth. For a second Li thought that he had seen her climb up from the dive platform. No – the ends of the sofa would have obscured his view.

She hid her face in her hair and headed for the door that led away from the far corner. The man turned back to his cards.

The door led to a wood-panelled dining area. A big mahogany table was surrounded by chairs upholstered in the same purple as the sofa. It was empty. At the end of the dining room were two doors. One of them had a small porthole and she could see through to the galley, where the inky head of a Filipino chef was bent over a steaming pot.

The other door led into a corridor. Li crept along and into a tiny hallway with metal stairs and another door, which she opened gently. A cabin – one single bed and another bed on the wall above that could be pulled down. The sheets were rumpled and a few items of clothing lay strewn on the chairs. They looked like the whites the chef was wearing. This must be his cabin.

She came out again. The engine noise was louder in the hallway, suggesting that the stairs led down to the engines. She decided she'd investigate there if she didn't find Bowman elsewhere, but first she retraced her steps through the dining room and the saloon. The guard was still playing Patience. He looked up as she went past.

'Are you lost?' he said.

Li rattled off some words of Mandarin, hoping he wouldn't understand, or at least that he wouldn't realize it wasn't Filipino. He looked back at her and shrugged. But she had seen what she had been looking for – a set of steps leading down from the corner of the saloon, guarded by a brass rail. She pattered down, her tray held high.

At the bottom there was a choice: right or left. Hearing a door open, she paused. A man in a cream-coloured linen shirt and white trousers came out and she recognized him immediately: Neil Hearst. The floor rocked slightly under her feet.

He saw her. 'I'll have those,' he said. 'Come this way.' He didn't look at her face at all, simply accepting her as part of the furniture.

She followed him into a little vestibule like the entrance to a hotel room, then the room opened out into a suite. It was in a terrible mess and it smelled stale. A double bed had been made roughly, another bunk had been pulled out of the wall and a sofa had also been used as a bed. Clothes and towels were strewn on the floor. It looked as if three people had been sleeping in that one room.

On the sofa was the man she was looking for: Bill Bowman.

Hearst motioned for her to put the drinks down on a coffee table in front of the sofa. She obeyed, trying to take in as much detail about Bowman as possible. He was wearing the same clothes as he had on the night of the attempted assassination – so Li concluded that he'd been kidnapped that same evening. The jacket of the suit lay discarded on the back of the sofa and he was in his shirtsleeves. He looked tired, a resigned expression in his eyes – the typical look of the prisoner. Li wanted to give him a sign to indicate that she was there to help, but she couldn't. The most important thing she could do was assess whether he would be fit enough to escape. What about this illness the press office had mentioned? Was that real or just a smokescreen to explain his disappearance? It was hard to tell. Li silently apologized as she gave Bowman the used glass with its nasty mixture of orange juice and whatever else.

There were more glasses on the table and several ashtrays. As she loaded them onto her tray, she glimpsed papers underneath: some long paragraphs beginning with numbers; a sentence that went, *whereas the contractor ArBonCo (known hereafter as 'the contractor').*

It was some kind of legal agreement. Was this what Amber had heard Simon Ter Haar talking about – the agreement that Bowman had to sign and that would also be his death warrant?

She moved one of the papers to pick up a wet coaster. It revealed further papers underneath.

These papers contained a set of signatures.

Bowman had already signed.

There was something else there too. A piece of paper with a few lines typed on it and Bowman's signature beneath. Li tried to read it as fast as she could.

Forgive me. In time, Curaçao will recover. But I cannot live with the shame.

A suicide note. Li swallowed.

She finished clearing and left. It was a relief to get out. The staleness was oppressive.

There were no guards with Bowman at the moment; there probably didn't need to be – there was nowhere to go. Most likely they only had the one guard upstairs to wave a gun at anyone who misbehaved. Or to execute troublemakers.

She slipped into the next cabin. She needed to know every inch so that she could establish escape routes and possible hiding places. The cabin was big and opulent, like the previous one, but in mirror image. A navy blue silk dressing gown was draped over the end of the bed. She pulled open the wardrobe – shirts, linen trousers, deck shoes. This must be Hearst's cabin. In the bathroom was a handsome shaving brush. She had a quick look in his bathroom cabinet. Shaving foam and aftershave – plus various glass and plastic bottles. One of them caught her eye. She took it down and read the label. Temazepam. Sleeping pills. The bottle was full, so it didn't look as though Hearst used them a lot. In fact, it was surprising that Hearst used them at all: the rest of the cupboard was filled with vitamin pills. Why were they here?

Down in the water, Alex waited. The time dragged. He seemed to be checking his watch every three minutes.

Li had now been on board for about half an hour.

He heard the thrumming of an engine. After a few minutes a shadow slid over the brilliant blue surface. A boat was pulling up, a smallish motorboat the same size as the *Fathom Sprite*. It docked next to the boarding platform. Someone was coming aboard. Who? While he'd been down there counting the minutes Alex had conjured in his head a design for an unobtrusive periscope, but now he wished he had one for real. He'd have to get what clues he could.

Someone's weight dipped the boarding platform, making Li's gear swing. It only did it the once.

So, one person had come aboard.

A soft boom nearby in the water shook Alex for a moment, then he got himself together. That was Li's signal. A flash-bang on a long burn, attached to a paperweight.

Alex swam up to the hull, where Li's sea scooter hung, and attached his own scooter to the same set of magnets.

A big white shape cruised past. A shark. Li's boom must have attracted it. Alex's breathing inside the closed system grew rapid and loud. He forced it to slow. The shark would probably ignore him. But if he didn't calm down and concentrate on the mission he might make a mistake.

He slipped off his BCD gear, hanging it up with Li's, and pulled himself onto the boarding platform.

Behind him the motorboat rocked gently on the water.

Footsteps on the deck above! Alex shrank against the bulkhead. He was still wearing his wetsuit and hood, which would be a dead giveaway. They had decided there was no point in him bringing a disguise; with his fair colouring he obviously couldn't pass as a servant. If someone came down to the boat he would have to tumble into the water.

Slim legs in slip-on shoes reached over for the ladder. Li.

She pattered down and crouched next to him.

'You're well hidden,' she whispered. 'I couldn't see you from up there.'

Alex had loads of questions, but he had to get a swift and complete picture of the set-up first. 'How many are aboard?'

'Two with guns, one who was in the saloon and one who has just come aboard. He's the hit man we saw earlier at Ter Haar's. Otherwise there's Hearst, Bowman, a chef, a couple of maids and a captain and first mate on the bridge. But the staff are nothing to do with this, they're just running the boat.'

Alex groaned. 'We're up against the man who tried to drown Amber? I don't like the sound of that.'

Li was already thinking ahead. 'Bowman's signed. I'm sure they're going kill him now.'

'Where is he?'

'Down below in a cabin.'

'How many exits?'

Li shook her head. 'We can't sneak him out like that. But we won't have to. I don't think they're going to kill him here. They're going to drug him with sleeping pills and put him in the boat and take him somewhere.'

'Why?'

'Who knows? Perhaps Hearst doesn't want his upholstery ruined.'

'No,' said Alex, thinking hard. 'I reckon they want the body found. If they dump him here the body would break up and be eaten before it ever got back to shore. They need to have him identified as dead.'

Li nodded. 'That explains it. They could just shoot him here, but then he might never be found. With the sleeping pills, it will look like suicide.'

Alex looked at her. 'Why do you think that's what they're going to do?'

Li grimaced. 'I found the pills – and a suicide note. And Hearst has just sent me to fetch a bottle of water. '"Mr Bowman wants a long drink,"' he said.

Alex looked at her. 'You sound like you have a plan.'

Li nodded. 'I have. You need to get back in the water.'

20

STAND BY

'I've got Alex's trace,' said Hex. 'He's out of the water.'

Paulo was leaning back dozing, soaking up the last rays of the afternoon sun. 'Now we just have to wait for Li's signal. Amber, are you sure all boats have satellite phones?'

Amber was looking brighter. 'Of course they do.'

Paulo sat up. He couldn't doze now. If Li had called Alex out of the water, the operation had moved on a phase. They were no longer doing reconnaissance, they were about to take action. 'Hex, are you sure we're not in a dead zone?' he checked.

'We're out in the open water,' said Hex patiently. 'There are satellites above us. There are no dead zones.' Beside him was a satellite phone, borrowed from Danny.

Amber felt her insides churn, but this time it wasn't because of the oil she had swallowed. She remembered the man who had tried to drown her, his cold persistence as he chased her through the plantation, his ruthless expression as he watched her dive. They were up against dangerous people, and the sickness she felt now was fear for her friends.

Alex slipped back into the water and under the boarding platform. Over his shoulder was a loop of rope which he had taken from the deck. He put his diving gear on and hung the rope on the washing line between the magnets, next to Li's diving kit. He had to work quickly; he didn't know how much time he would have. Pulling one of the magnets free, then the other, he swooped down, came up under the blue hull of the motorboat and fixed the magnets to the underside.

Now Li's dive gear was attached to the motorboat. The rebreather unit was no longer of any use – underwater, it was immediately soaked and useless – so the emergency air supply tanks were vital to the plan and Alex took special care to check they were firmly attached. He slipped off the loop of rope and then swam to the stern of the boat. The propeller hung down on the stalk from the engine, like a big electric fan. He tried not to think of it starting up – the sound of his breathing was so loud that he couldn't tell if there was anyone in the boat – but in his mind's eye he could see his hands and face disappearing in a blur of ripped flesh. Quickly he threw the rope over the engine, round the arm that connected it to the hull, then knotted it and let the rope unfurl into the water. Now he had to test the knot. The propeller was now right beside his cheek, so close that he could see the rust spots on the blades and the scratches in the paintwork. He started to feel queasy all over again – funny how the silliest thing could bring you out in a cold sweat. But he made sure he tested the rope. No sense in not doing it properly.

Relieved, he swam out of harm's way, leaving the rope trailing down into the water. From the surface, no one would be able to see it.

So far so good. He'd done all the essentials. He had a number of other items to secure but that was just to make life easier.

Soon the two sea scooters also hung from the bottom of the boat.

Now he had to wait again.

For the second time Li descended the stairs with a tray. On it was a bottle of water from the bar plus an empty glass on a paper coaster. She made her way to the cabin where Bowman was being held.

She pushed open the door and the stale air hit her like the blast from an oven. Hearst was in there with Bowman, plus the guard she had seen on the main deck and the hit man who had chased Amber. The hit man had a pistol in his lap. Li put the tray down.

Hearst turned to Bowman. 'We can do this the hard way, Bill, or are you going to make it easy for yourself?'

Bowman looked at his captors. 'If you don't mind, I think I'll have them with a glass of water.'

Hearst waved his hand towards Li in an imperious way. 'Pour.'

Li unscrewed the top of the water and poured it into the glass. She could see the bottle of sleeping pills on the floor by the arm of the sofa. As she filled the tumbler right up, she felt like she was committing murder herself. She slid the tray across to Bowman, leaving the glass on its coaster. Hearst bent down and picked up the bottle of pills and poured out a heap. There must have been at least twenty – a massive dose. He pushed them across the table. 'Down the hatch, Bill.'

Bowman picked up some pills and looked at them.

'You said you wanted it the easy way, Bill,' said the hit man. He fingered the pistol.

Bowman seemed to decide he had no choice. He took two pills, then lifted the glass and washed them down with some water. The paper coaster was still stuck to the bottom of the glass. Li tried not to stare at it, her heart pounding faster. Would the others see what she had done?

The hit man spoke. 'Neil,' he said curtly, 'we don't want witnesses.'

Hearst twitched his head in the direction of the door. Li understood. She turned to go.

But while they were looking at her they hadn't been looking at Bowman. He had peeled the coaster off the bottom of the glass and crumpled it into his trouser pocket.

Good. He'd taken it. That meant he'd read the message Li had written on it. And he'd got the spare tracer, stuck on the coaster.

Li left the room and ran up the steps to the lounge. There was no time to waste. On a low table next to the sofa was a satellite phone. She picked it up and dialled.

Paulo answered. 'Yes?'

It was so good to hear his voice. Li used Spanish, in case she was overheard. 'I've got to be quick. Can you see the tracers?'

'*Si*,' said Paulo. 'We've got two, but Alex's has disappeared.'

'OK, here's what you've got to do.'

* * *

Amber and Hex looked quizzically at Paulo as he finished the phone call.

'Who's this third trace?' said Hex.

'Why doesn't Alex's show?' said Amber. 'They were both on the boat.'

'The third trace is Bowman,' said Paulo. 'Li has given him the spare. Alex's has gone because he's underwater again. This is the plan. Bowman's will start moving soon and we need to shadow it in the boat – but not get too close. Alex will be with the boat all the way. They're going to drug Bowman, put him in the motorboat and dump him somewhere near to land so that he's washed up dead. He'll have at least one armed guard, possibly two.'

Amber shuddered. 'My old friend the hit man, no doubt. What do we do about them?'

'We don't,' said Paulo. 'When we see Bowman's trace move, we make sure we're nearby, but we don't actually go in to get him until we see it disappear again. That means the hit man has thrown him overboard and he's in the water – with Alex. The hit man goes, and we pick Bowman and Alex up.'

The others nodded, taking it in.

'What if the hit man decides to stove in Bowman's skull for good measure?' asked Amber quietly. 'That'll kill him before we even have a chance to rescue him.'

Paulo answered. 'They wouldn't bother with the sleeping pills then,' he said.

'We hope,' said Amber.

'What about Li?' said Hex, thinking carefully.

'She's staying on the boat,' said Paulo. 'We go and get her afterwards. When Bowman's trace disappears we need to move in fast. Alex will be using the emergency air supply and he and Bowman will run out of air quickly.'

Li was in the galley. The chef was chopping meat, while she was up the other end, pretending to wash glasses behind the bar. If anyone came along she could duck down so that she wasn't seen.

She had been there for nearly an hour when she heard heavy footsteps on the stairs. Several sets, moving clumsily as though carrying something awkward. She looked through the window. Hearst, carrying a diver's weight belt, was in front, followed by the hit man, his head and shoulders appearing first. He was walking backwards.

As he reached the top of the stairs, Li could see that he was carrying Bowman, his arms hooked in Bowman's armpits. Bowman's head lolled, his eyes closed and his arms hanging limply. Coming up from below was the other guard, supporting the feet. They manoeuvred the awkward weight past the galley, Bowman swinging between them like a heavy hammock.

Li watched them for as long as she dared over the top of the counter, then ducked down out of sight. She didn't need to see any more. It had begun.

21

Bowman

Alex felt the boat rock as someone – the hit man? – got into it and found their balance. Feet were moving about on the boarding platform above. There was a scraping noise and the boat dipped. Something heavy had just been loaded.

Hanging just a couple of metres under the boat, Alex gave a final glance at the equipment hanging from the bottom of the boat. It should hold.

The boat tipped slightly towards the rear as the hit man moved to start the engine. But the boat didn't rock nearly as much as when he had been on board on his own; his weight was counterbalanced by something. Bowman's dead weight in the bottom.

Alex hoped that Li had managed to carry out her part of the plan.

The engine spluttered into life. In moments they would be on the move. Alex made sure of his grip on the rope. Then the propeller bit and the boat accelerated. He found himself streaming behind in its wake like a fallen water skier, his weight belt keeping him a few metres below the water line. At first he could barely do more than hang on for dear life. But bit by bit he got used to it. It was like being a torpedo.

So long as they carried on at this speed, it was good; it meant that the hit man was oblivious to the cargo he carried below. Alex prayed it would stay that way.

'Hey, guys,' said Hex. 'That's Bowman. Time we were on the move.' He rattled off the co-ordinates to Amber and she started the engine, checking her compass to ensure they were on the right course.

Paulo was looking at the other trace on Hex's screen: Li, still on the *Black Gold*.

'She can look after herself for a while,' said Amber. 'It's Bowman who needs our help first.'

Paulo nodded. Li was resourceful, brave and kicked like a mule. But she was staying in the lion's den and he couldn't help but feel uneasy.

The sun was setting. They'd been out there for a long time, waiting and worrying.

The hit man sped away from the *Black Gold*. He had a particular spot in mind, where the currents would take Bowman into land. On the floor of the boat lay a large shape covered by a tarpaulin – Bowman, hidden from view in case anyone came past and looked in. People who had been given sleeping pills in large quantities generally looked pretty ill; in fact, there was a risk that Bowman might die before he got him into the water. If so, all well and good.

All was going to plan, but one tiny thing surprised him. It was taking quite a bit of throttle to get the boat up to speed. Surely Bowman wasn't *that* heavy. Reaching the position he had aimed for, he checked his hand-held GPS and cut the engine. The boat drifted.

He kneeled in the boat, got his hands under Bowman's shoulders, tarpaulin and all, and heaved, lifting him up onto the edge of the boat. His head flopped into the water. The hit man tipped the rest of him in quickly, in case the cold water brought him round. As he did so, something fell out of Bowman's pocket. The hit man gave it barely a glance; it looked like a small coin.

Bowman sank, the green tarpaulin billowing up and distorting as if it was boiling. The weight belt ensured he sank quickly and he was soon out of sight.

The hit man turned away. Time to go.

The small silver tracer glinted in the sunlight on the floor of the boat.

Alex had to act fast. As soon as the hit man cut the engine, he was ready. Sure enough, the boat began to rock as the hit man prepared to throw Bowman's body overboard.

Alex let go of the rope and rapidly pulled the magnets off the hull while the boat was rocking above him. He let the two scooters drift slowly down. A head and shoulders appeared over the side of the boat, a trail of bubbles coming from the lips. Alex would have to work fast.

Moments later Bowman was floating down, the tarpaulin cocooned around him. Alex swam strongly towards him. It was like catching someone falling from a high building in slow motion; every second counted. His hand met the tarpaulin and he thrust it aside. Where was Bowman's face? He couldn't find it. The tarpaulin was like a giant, live curtain, moving with a mind of its own. He could feel something inside it struggling, but whenever he grabbed at it he only caught empty material. What if Bowman died here and now because Alex wasn't quick enough?

Then Alex saw Bowman's face; his mouth and eyes shut in tight lines. Tiny bubbles were escaping from his mouth. Alex pushed the regulator of Li's emergency air supply into Bowman's mouth and pinched the man's nose to force him to breathe correctly through it.

He waited. Was Bowman still conscious?

Suddenly, the big man came to life, his hands

flying to the regulator. He began to take big, desperate gulps.

Alex had Li's mask on his arm. He put it over Bowman's face and the man took over, adjusting the mask so that it was comfortable. Alex relaxed. Bowman was OK and, what's more, he knew how to handle the equipment. Alex handed him Li's BCD and Bowman struggled into it.

It was only then that Alex realized he could stop worrying about the plan. It had worked. Li had successfully managed to swap the sleeping pills with Neil Hearst's vitamins.

Alex scribbled on his slate. *Friend*. He pointed to himself.

Bowman gave him a thumbs-up. The tarpaulin fell away from him like a cloak. He looked rather comical underwater in his shirt and suit trousers, making Alex think of a stunt man.

Wait here, he wrote on the slate. Then he dived down after the sea scooters, powering like mad with his fins to catch them up as they sank into the deep blue. He grabbed them and pulled them back up. Glancing up to the surface, he checked that the motorboat had gone. The hit man thought he had done his job. Bowman was safe – for now.

But there was another problem to contend with. They didn't have much air. Li's rebreather obviously couldn't be used because the mouthpiece was wet – which also meant they couldn't buddy-breathe with Alex's. After Li's emergency tank ran out, there was Alex's own emergency supply and that was it. Twenty minutes' air total.

He wished they could get moving themselves, but he didn't know how far they were from the shore. Anyway, while they were underwater, the others couldn't see their trace, so swimming off would be pointless. Since the team had his co-ordinates from when the boat had stopped, they knew their position and would be coming. They had to stay where they were and just wait.

He hoped they would come quickly.

'Surely,' said Amber, 'the trace should have gone. He should be out of the boat and underwater with Alex by now.' She pulled on a pink sweater. Now the sun had set, it was colder.

Hex zipped up his black fleece. 'It's about ten seconds since you last asked. Look, it's still moving.' He showed her the screen. The small dot that was the tracer Bowman was wearing when loaded onto the motorboat was still moving steadily.

'I don't like it, it's taking too long,' said Paulo.

'Bowman hasn't gone in yet,' said Hex steadily. 'We'll see the trace vanish when he does.'

They settled back to wait.

Alex looked at his dive computer. They'd been waiting for ten minutes. He checked the dial on Bowman's tank. Nearly empty. He quickly pulled his own off his BCD and set it up so that Bowman could switch to his emergency tank. Bowman gave him a worried look; clearly he knew that air tanks weren't supposed to run out that quickly.

Alex stayed calm; he had to give him confidence. But as he swapped the tank it was like a final countdown starting. Ten minutes and then that was it – they would have to surface and take their chances. In the open water, even with the small scooters, they could be swept around by the current.

Their strength would go and they would be far more at risk of drowning. Down here they had more control.

He looked into the miles of sea around him and the blue glowing surface and wished he could conjure up the white boat. Had something gone wrong? The sea scooters hung below him on their lanyards, drifting gently in the current. How far away was the bottom? The green tarpaulin had vanished, tumbled away into the blue. Had it floated all the way down or was it still going? Alex shuddered. He felt very alone.

Bowman pointed to Alex's slate and pencil. He wanted to write a message. Alex handed them over and Bowman drew a noughts and crosses grid, then put an X in the middle to start a game.

Alex took the slate back and marked a nought in the bottom left-hand corner before handing it back. He hoped they wouldn't have to play for very long.

22

WAITING GAME

Li loaded some glasses onto a tray. She had to keep busy, stay inconspicuous.

The *Black Gold* was quiet, just as it had been before. You'd hardly guess that the occupants had just sent a man to his death.

She kept doing sums in her head. It was about half an hour since the hit man had left with Bowman. The others had to pick Bowman up first – so it would probably be another twenty minutes to half an hour before they got to her. The waiting was hard.

The same set of thoughts kept going round in her head. Maybe she should grab one of the yacht's jet skis and make a run for it. No, that was silly; she wouldn't know where to go; nor did she know how much fuel they had. The ocean was a big place to get lost in, and if her escape attempt failed, she would have blown her cover. No, she had to stick to the plan: stay and wait for the others.

At least it should be easier now they didn't have to get Alex and Bowman off. Hex and Paulo could sweep in close on their own jet skis and she could slip into the water and just wait for them to get close enough for her to climb on too. The jet skiers would look like tourists on holiday, coming over to the yacht out of simple curiosity. It should be simple.

Better do something. She took the tray of glasses out of the galley and into the dining room. Neil Hearst was there, kneeling in front of one of the cupboards. He hadn't seen her. She froze, her sixth sense telling her to stay hidden. Inside the cupboard was a safe. He twisted the dial to and fro to open it, then put in a sheaf of papers tied with pink legal ribbon. Finally he closed it.

Li ducked back into the galley, her heart pounding in time with the pot bubbling on the stove. There was only one thing those papers could be – the documents Bill Bowman had been forced to sign.

It hadn't occurred to her before to go for the documents, but here she was with time on her hands. And she knew where they were. If she could take them, they would be very useful evidence.

If she *could*.

Sometimes it seemed as though Li wasn't in command of her skills – they were in charge of her. Without thinking, she'd memorized the combination of the safe.

But first she needed to take the glasses to the dining room.

Bowman drew the last stroke of a stick figure hanging from a gallows. They were now playing Hangman. Alex had run out of lives trying to guess the word.

Bowman wiped out what was on the slate, then wrote three dashes.

Alex decided to try guessing a whole word instead of individual letters. Reaching for the slate, he wrote *Oil*, then passed it back.

Bowman drew the first part of the scaffold. Not right.

Alex tried again. He was a bit rusty on technique. The last time he'd played had been a few years back at school. He had certainly never thought he'd find himself underwater, waiting for rescue and playing Hangman with a man whose life he'd just saved.

Bowman was waiting for an answer. Alex wrote: *E*.

Bowman put an *E* in the middle of the word. Alex could have sworn that inside the mask the grey eyes were twinkling with amusement.

Alex suddenly twigged. *Wet!* he wrote.

Bowman gave him a thumbs-up.

Alex's turn. Words he didn't really want to share leaped unbidden into his head. *Time*, and *Air*. No, he thought. Paulo and the others had to be on their way. He knew the tracers worked. Still, he looked at his dive computer again. Bowman only had about seven more minutes of air and now there wasn't much left in Alex's rebreather either. He'd had to spend far more time underwater than they'd originally planned for.

Bowman was waiting. Alex marked out a five-letter word.

E, Bowman guessed.

Alex wrote it in. Bowman thought for a moment, then seemed to read Alex's mind. *Steak*, he tried.

Alex grinned; his turn to give a thumbs-up.

Bowman took the slate again and marked five spaces. Without hesitation, Alex took it back and wrote *Chips*. Bowman nodded vigorously. The two of them hung there laughing, diver style, air hoses pulsing, Alex's torch wobbling, bubbles shooting out of Bowman's regulator.

Alex stopped, but Bowman seemed to carry on just as intensely. Something didn't look right; Bowman was patting his chest, thumping it as though in discomfort.

Alex felt like the water around him had turned to ice. Was the oil chief having a heart attack? They had to surface. He grabbed the slate and wrote: *Stay calm. Breathe OUT.*

Bowman nodded, his grey eyes wide behind the mask.

The BCDs had an emergency cord. Alex pulled Bowman's then his own and the BCDs inflated like lifejackets, shooting both of them upwards. It was all Alex could do to remember to breathe out as they rose rapidly through the water. He hoped Bowman had; if he breathed in, he could burst something in his lungs.

Moments later they were on the surface and the world suddenly became loud and wide. The scooters hung down, dragging in the water. With the BCD holding him up, Alex didn't have to tread water but waves were splashing in his face. He kept his mask on so he could see but pulled off his mouthpiece and swam to Bowman. He pulled Bowman's mask up and put it on his forehead – the diver's signal for trouble. Bowman was breathing hard now, still clutching his chest. Alex's own heart was doing somersaults. Would Bowman die out here after all?

Alex didn't know what to do about heart attacks, but he did know that it was always important to keep the airway open. He turned Bowman onto his back and tilted his head back, the way he'd been taught in Duke of Edinburgh Award life-saving sessions. Bowman coughed and spluttered, his eyes rolling, his breathing harsh and ragged. He was trying to swim. Alex put his arms around him to steady him. 'Keep still,' he said. 'The lifejackets will keep us afloat. Rescue will be here soon.'

Bowman nodded. Alex could feel him trying to relax, but every now and again a spasm passed through his chest. Alex felt his legs twitch and kick in the water.

'Have you had this before?' Alex asked. But a spasm gripped Bowman and he couldn't answer.

What if Bowman stopped breathing? Alex wondered if he could give the kiss of life, out there in the water. He looked around at the horizon. It was dark. He hadn't noticed while they were underwater, but night was falling fast. They were out in the sea, in the dark. If they weren't picked up soon, they were bound to die.

Bowman relaxed.

'Has it gone?' Alex asked him.

Bowman nodded. His eyes were wide; frightened.

'Is it your chest?' Alex asked.

Bowman shook his head. It was as if he was afraid to talk in case he set off the pain again. Still, at least he didn't look as if he was suffering for the moment.

Alex patted his jacket. The torch still hung off it. He flashed it around. It still worked. If he saw any boats nearby at least he had something to signal with.

He shortened the lanyard so that it held the torch near his face, then froze. There was a white triangle sticking out of the water, like a tooth.

Not a tooth. A fin.

A shark.

Of course. Sharks were drawn to feeble, weak movements – they thought it was something dying. Bowman's thrashing must have attracted one. And it was evening.

Feeding time.

23

VICTORY

Li kneeled by the safe. Her fingers worked quickly on the dial, twisting it back and forth until she heard a faint click as the tumblers dropped into place and she felt the door release. She'd done it. She was in.

She pulled the heavy door open and pulled out the documents, then swiftly closed it again. She heard a noise behind her and got to her feet, picking up the tray and holding it over the papers.

Hearst was standing by the door when she got there, his arm barring the way. Had he seen her? No. He wasn't looking at the tray. Or even her face.

He was looking at her legs in the short black dress.

Li kept her eyes down. That way she'd look shy – and maybe he'd think she didn't understand. She nodded in the direction of the galley, as though trying to indicate she needed to go back there.

Hearst let her pass, but she could feel his eyes on her as she went.

Luckily the galley was empty. Li slipped inside and stood to the side of the door, hoping that Hearst would assume that the chef would be in there too. Once he'd gone she'd slip out.

But for now she had the documents.

Alex had the sea scooter in front of him, Bowman clinging onto his waist. As they zoomed through the water they made a wake like a small boat. A spray of seawater washed over them like a constant tidal wave. Alex's ears buzzed; the scooter made a noise like a drill on the surface.

The shark's fin was still alongside them. It was matching his speed. He would have to do more.

He turned roughly in a big circle. The shark carried on, its fin zipping past him, like a saw through the water. Alex turned even more sharply and the scooter almost wrenched his arms out of their sockets. He held on for dear life and powered out of the turn.

Bowman gripped his waist even tighter. Alex felt him curling up – had the pain hit him again? Heart attacks could be brought on by stress – and this wasn't likely to help matters. 'Sorry, mate,' he muttered under his breath. 'It's this or be eaten by the shark.'

He glanced up. The shark was further away. He knew sharks could swim fast but he also knew they weren't very manoeuvrable.

Bowman's grip was slipping from around his waist. Alex wanted to pull him up like a slipping garment but he didn't dare let go – the sea scooter was so powerful he needed all his strength to control it. Then Bowman coughed and tightened his hold.

The shark was coming for them again. Alex whipped around in another circle, holding onto the handlebars like grim death. He felt his legs wave out like the back end of a car.

Bowman slipped away.

In the constant noise, the constant wash of fast water, it took Alex a few moments to realize there were no longer arms hanging onto him. He cut the throttle and looked round.

And thought he was seeing a mirage. On the water, lit by glowing torches, was a jumble of figures. They separated into two jet skis with riders. One rider was leaning into the water and hoisting Bowman out. The other was coming towards him.

A strong pair of arms topped by a head of curly hair leaned down like a circus rider and pulled Alex out of the water. Alex grabbed the back seat of the jet ski and clambered on. The two sea scooters dangled from him, bumping against the hull as Paulo pulled away.

Alex leaned forward and yelled in Paulo's ear, 'Get going – shark!'

Paulo grinned back at him. 'Believe me, *hombre*, I've seen it.' But as they glanced towards the sinister fin, they could see it was moving away. Now they were on the jet skis, they could outrun it.

Hex was already racing off ahead towards a white boat: the *Fathom Sprinter*, controlled by Amber. He was struggling to keep upright as his passenger leaned and swayed.

'You must be Bill,' Hex shouted over his shoulder.

His only reply was a ragged cough. Hex looked round: Bowman was clutching his chest; he didn't look good. Hex twisted the throttle as far as it would go. They had to get back and call the coastguard. Fast.

Li walked into the saloon with a tray of glasses. Under the tray was the contract, hidden from view.

Hearst was in there. He didn't acknowledge her, but went straight to the satellite phone and pressed a button. Then he listened, looking puzzled. Li's mouth went dry. That was redial; it would probably get him the satellite phone in the *Fathom Sprinter*. Hearst pressed cancel and hit redial again. Li tried to look as though she was taking no notice. If Paulo or one of the others did answer he wouldn't know who it was.

She moved out to the sun deck. There was a set of white-painted metal steps leading up to the deck above. She hadn't been up there yet, but she could see another table and chairs. If she took the glasses up there it would keep her on the move until Paulo and Hex arrived.

She climbed the steps. The breeze was fresh up on this deck. Maybe it was a good place to wait – she'd be able to spot any approaching lights and she could see the bridge, and the dark-skinned captain looking at a row of green, glowing instruments.

Somebody came up the stairs and she looked behind her. Hearst. What did he want?

He smiled – that nasty, ingratiating smile. Li smiled back.

His expression changed. Why? She suddenly realized. Coming up from below, he could see she had papers under the tray – papers tied with pink legal ribbon. His eyes became flinty. He climbed the stairs, his eyes fixed on hers.

'I think,' he said, 'you have something of mine.'

24

UNMASKED

Hearst came up onto the deck. 'You know what I find fascinating about you? For a Filipino you have excellent teeth. I didn't think any of you activists would have the nerve to actually come to my boat, but here you are.' He put out his hand. 'Hand the documents over.'

Li threw the tray at him. She heard the glasses smash but already she was vaulting over the rail and onto the deck below, the folder tucked under one arm.

She landed like a cat, and glimpsed a movement

through the window of the saloon – the commotion had alerted someone. She was moving in seconds. She had to get to the jet skis.

She ran for the launch platform, hurdling the canvas chairs. Beside her, there was a hiss of compressed air and a ripping sound. A vicious-looking arrow shot into the canvas of the chair just ahead of her. They were firing at her with the harpoon.

Li vaulted down onto the platform. Another harpoon whistled past, so close she could feel it on her face.

She released a jet ski and it hit the dark water with a splash. She squeezed the contract down the top of her wetsuit and jumped on. The jet ski wobbled and she grabbed the handlebars to stop herself falling, just as a figure loomed over the steps to the launch platform, a slender rod in his hand. The harpoon gun. She had to get away before he fired again.

Li started the engine and roared off. The jet ski wasn't like the ones she'd used earlier; this kind had no seat – you stood up on it like a scooter.

Behind her, another jet ski hit the water. The wail

of the engine came in stereo. But there was another noise too. Gunfire.

Someone was shooting at her. With bullets.

She glanced behind. Two lights were haring around on the water – two jet skis now after her.

Headlights; she hadn't realized the jet ski had headlights. She turned hers on and they illuminated a small triangle of choppy navy blue water ahead of her, but they also spoiled her night vision. She turned them off; she was probably better off without them. As she pushed the throttle up to full speed, the machine pulled away like a turbo-charged motorbike. These were serious performance vehicles.

Either side of her, out of the corners of both eyes, she could see the lights of the other jet skis. They were gaining on her, trying to cut her off.

She pulled the handlebars to one side, then the other. The bike slalomed through the water from side to side like a skier down a mountain. Two headlights followed her, veering to head her off. Their lights were like beacons homing in on her. The sound of jet skis was everywhere, echoing off the water – it sounded as though there were a hundred of them.

She made the corners sharper to give them something to think about but misjudged one and found herself sliding along at ninety degrees, one side in the sea. She put her foot out on the water as though it was a solid surface, then righted herself and carried on. She still had the contract safe, stuffed down her wetsuit. It would have been fun if she hadn't been fleeing for her life.

She glanced back, hoping one of the jet skiers behind would fall, but both headlights continued to pursue her doggedly. The gunfire came again. She slalomed, forcing her pursuers to do the same. While they were sliding like that, they couldn't aim. She made the slaloms more and more extreme, leaning further over each time.

Li could feel the surface of the water becoming increasingly choppy. It was now like riding over bumpy hills. But they seemed to be able to follow her, no matter what she did.

Time for a different tactic.

She stopped and swerved around 180 degrees so she was facing them, throwing up a great wave like a flourish.

She had to do this before they had time to fire.

Hearst and his guard saw the slight girl pull the papers out of her wetsuit and rip them in half. She threw her arm up in a big arc and the torn papers scattered into the water. Then she was off.

Li looked behind her. Papers were floating on the surface of the water, bobbing on the waves. Hearst and the guard were trying to gather them up before the ink ran too much.

Then she heard a roar behind her. A moment later came the sounds of shots. The chase was on again. Li put the jet ski into a spectacular slide, travelling ten metres sideways with her foot on the water. Behind her, one of the jet skis went over completely then bounced upright, the engine idling while it turned in a circle. Only one to go now. And he wasn't shooting. Good – perhaps she'd made things more even.

She pointed the nose of the jet ski down into the water. The jet ski began to dive. How far would it go? Li committed to the move and went with it. For a moment she was completely submerged, then she came up again like a dolphin.

A shot rang out. Something magenta-coloured

whizzed past her into the water. She thought she'd dealt with the gunman.

But now something else was in front of her, visible in the light of the other jet ski. A craft she recognized. The motorboat. With one occupant.

The hit man.

His boat was stationary and she was heading straight for it. The light of the pursuing jet ski illuminated a figure kneeling in the boat. He was aiming something and Li suddenly realized what the magenta glow had been. A flare. He was trying to shoot her with a flare pistol. It lacked refinement as a weapon, but would be more devastating at close range than a pistol.

He'd missed before but she was now so close that no matter how she swerved he would not miss. If it hit her it would blow a hole in her like an exploding firework.

Li steered straight, then pulled up and threw her weight to the side. The jet ski soared up, sliding along sideways – but not in the water, in the air. She flew right over the boat in something like a karate leap, then was engulfed by water.

She came up, spluttering, on the other side of the hit man's boat. Bobbing in the water beside her jet ski, she saw a magenta glow through the gloom, then an orange flash that ended in a muffled boom. The hit man had shot the other jet ski and its fuel tank had gone up. She could see his silhouette against the orange flames; the hit man was still in the boat, but no longer in firing position.

Li's engine had stopped. The air seemed so quiet without the roar of the jet skis and the fizz of moving water. Now there were new sounds to get used to – a *whump* of fuel burning and a man screaming. She stayed where she was, treading water. If she got up again, the hit man might see her. Her best hope was to hide by the jet ski and wait until he went away. She thanked her lucky stars she'd kept her headlights off, it was her best chance of not being seen.

That *whump* noise was getting louder.

It wasn't just the fuel burning.

It was a helicopter.

Then she saw them – the tail and nose lights of two helicopters. Suddenly they turned on searchlights – great triangular beams that swung around the dark water. One found the hit man's boat and fixed on him like an eye.

More lights appeared, this time at surface level. The whine of engines added to the orchestra of noises. One of the searchlights passed over them and illuminated three motorboats.

Who were they? Where had they all come from?

The hit man decided to run for it. He opened the throttle on his engine and swept away, one helicopter following him, its searchlight locked on; it wasn't letting him go. Li chuckled – the hit man looked like he was trying to escape being kidnapped by aliens.

A powerful light shone in her eyes. She put her hands up and squinted at the direction it had come from.

A silver dinghy puttered up beside her. 'Are you all right?' The torch tilted upwards so that she could see a face. Greg, the coastguard. Danny was there too. Their strong arms reached into the water to help her in.

Li kicked the few metres to the edge of the boat and caught the rope on the edge. Rescue. Now that she could stop fighting to stay afloat she suddenly felt exhausted. Her other hand was still on the jet ski, trying to pull it with her.

'If you rescue me,' pleaded Li, 'will you promise to rescue this too?'

'Forget her,' said a voice. 'Just get the jet ski.' Paulo's face appeared by Danny's shoulder.

Li relaxed and let them pull her into the boat. Paulo was ready with a warm blanket. He put it around her while Danny and Greg caught the jet ski and tethered it to a ring on the side of the dinghy.

The surface of the water was mayhem. Two motorboats were screaming into the distance, the helicopter following them. The other helicopter was still pursuing the hit man. Li shook her head, amazed. 'Who are all these other people?'

'The police. We had to get medical help for Bowman and they got involved too.'

Li's fight for her own survival had been so intense that she had momentarily forgotten everything else. 'You got him, did you?'

'Yeah. He'll be fine.'

25

HEALING

As the morning sun glittered on the sea, Paulo, Li, Alex and Hex walked slowly along the beach, spread out in a line like police searching a crime scene. They didn't talk, just walked, heads bowed, looking for dead birds washed up during the night. This was now as much a part of their morning routine as cleaning their teeth.

Li's foot touched a bird. She scooped it out of the sand and into the basket she carried. The sand was greyish. Below the first couple of centimetres it was darker but already fresh sand was coming in to cover the tainted layers, like skin closing over a wound. In time, the beach would become white again and the sea would bring only sand, not these drifting black remains.

But they didn't need the masks any more. The most volatile chemicals that irritated the lungs were gone. Gloves were the only protection they needed now. That was an improvement too.

Paulo was thinking that such a lot had changed since he had last done this. Just twenty-four hours ago Bowman had been a prisoner with two conspirators preparing to kill him and begin a course of action that would ruin the environment. And Mara had been held by the police for questioning over the assassination attempt. Now Bowman would make a statement to the police and the government's fraud department would go through ArBonCo's records with a fine-tooth comb. All the evidence Hex had found when he hacked in illegally would come out in the open. It would clear Mara and would put Neil Hearst in jail. But Paulo still puzzled about one thing – where the conspirators were going to get their haul of $50 million.

Alex was thinking about that too. But, he figured, you could never know everything. When his dad went on a mission with the Regiment, he was given a specific task – rescue this hostage, destroy this base, find this information. Sometimes he didn't know why but he had to focus on the job in hand. One of the strengths of Alpha Force was that they were a unit on their own; they found problems and they solved them. When they went into action, they knew what would happen if they failed. And that made success all the more sweet.

Amber came out onto the veranda, sipping a glass of water very slowly. As soon as she had put her trowel into the grey sand to remove a bird the oily smell had turned her stomach over again.

Hex had filled his basket. He brought it up onto the veranda and put it down while he fetched a black plastic sack. Something in it caught Amber's eye. On top was a pair of birds, their scrawny blackened necks twined together like betrothed swans. He had dug them out together so that they were united in death. It was so poignant, such a symbol of how helpless everyone had been when a few men got greedy. There was a rustle behind her. Hex was coming back with a sack, shaking it to find the opening. He flapped it again and it sent a waft of oil over to her. Her insides suddenly felt like a cola can being shaken hard. This was not good. With as much dignity as she could muster, she hurried into the bar.

Hex saw her rush by, hand over her mouth. 'Amber, are you OK?' he called. 'Do you need anything?' He watched as she sat down in a dark corner and pulled the zip down on her wetsuit to get cool. She began sipping water. Hex decided she was probably all right and went back to work, head down, carefully digging.

After a few minutes someone came out onto the veranda, put on some gloves, picked up a trowel and basket and walked down onto the beach. Surely Amber shouldn't be doing that, Hex thought, turning round.

Instead of her close-cropped hair and ebony arms he found himself looking at a head of silvery hair.

It looked up. Grey eyes met his.

Hex gulped. 'Mr Bowman?'

Bowman straightened up and grasped Hex's hand. His grip was warm and firm as he shook it. 'Nice to meet you properly. There wasn't really time for introductions before.'

That was an understatement. The last time they'd met, Hex had been trying to keep his balance on a jet ski as Bowman had clutched his chest and gasped behind him. Now he looked rested and well. Hex didn't know what to say. 'I thought you were having a heart attack,' he said, and then thought that was probably a bit tactless.

'Not a heart attack, just a touch of angina,' replied Bowman. 'Brought on by stress. I've had so many tests this morning I'm like a pincushion.'

Amber came out, her big brown eyes amazed. Bowman turned and offered her his hand. 'Miss Mayday, isn't it?'

Amber smiled and shook his hand firmly. The last time he'd seen her she'd been at the helm of the *Fathom Sprinter*, shrieking, 'Mayday!' into the radio. 'I'm Amber. You frightened the life out of me last night.'

The others had put their trowels and baskets

down. Alex stepped forward and shook Bowman's hand. 'I'm Alex. So this is what you look like without a mask and regulator.'

Bowman grinned. 'Any time you want to be thrashed at Hangman again, let me know.'

He spotted Paulo next and shook his hand. 'The other cameraman, eh, along with Hex? Mara showed me the video evidence you got at the drill site.'

At once they all said, 'Is Mara out of custody?'

'She certainly is,' said Bowman. He turned to Li. The last time she'd seen him he had been facing death. His face was serious. 'The brave little undercover maid,' he said quietly. 'Your note saved my life. I thought I was done for.'

'Note?' said Paulo.

'I slipped him a note on a coaster,' said Li. 'It said, *Play dead – take disc*. Then Hearst wouldn't know I'd swapped the pills.' She touched Bowman's arm. 'You did brilliantly, you were so brave to go along with it. And when you took the disc on the coaster, you were taking the tracer so we could keep tabs on you from that moment on.'

Bowman bent over and began to dig out a bird. 'You guys were the brave ones.'

Quietly, they went back to work.

Alex's patch was beside Bowman's. Working side by side brought back the sense of camaraderie he'd felt while waiting underwater with him. 'I knew Ian Davidson, your security chief,' he said. 'He was my dad's friend.'

Bowman removed a bird from its sandy tomb and placed it carefully in the basket. 'He was a good man. When Hearst and his thugs took me they had to take him too because they knew he'd come after me. The assassination attempt was a set-up, as I'm sure you have realized. I wasn't supposed to die, just disappear. They took me and Ian to the yacht immediately. Hearst tried to make me sign that contract but I wouldn't. We never left that cabin – until Ian jumped the guard and got out. I don't know what happened but there was a terrible scuffle and I heard shots. Then they took me up to the main deck and showed me his body. I thought that was it. Ian had kept me going. Without him there, I had no choice but to sign. I thought they'd won . . .' His voice trailed off.

The others had put their trowels down, fascinated and appalled.

Amber was sitting on the veranda, her chin propped on her hands. 'Ian made a mayday call when he escaped. Because of that, we knew where to find you. So he carried on doing his job, right to the last minute. He saved you, really.'

They worked quietly for a while in companionable silence, turning over sand, lifting out blackened remains.

Bowman emptied his basket and came back to dig again. 'I'm going to talk to my lawyer about that contract. I want to make sure there's nothing that can be done with it.'

Li straightened up and tried to scratch an itch on her cheek with the back of her hand. 'There's no need. I got it.'

Bowman looked at her, incredulous. 'Did you?'

'From his safe. I was going to bring it back but I had to use it to distract Hearst. I left him picking up little pieces of it from all over the water.'

Bowman chuckled. 'I'd like to have seen that. He's a slimy double-crossing toad. I'd worked with him for ten years. We'd had our differences, but that doesn't excuse what he did. He didn't care how many lives he ruined; he just wanted to make a profit. Nature has given us a priceless resource and we should use it wisely . . .' He lifted out another bird. 'Sorry. I just got my campaigning hat on then for a moment.'

Paulo was working his way closer to Bowman's patch. 'Why do you think he did it?'

'He was frustrated because I stood in his way,' said Bowman simply. 'And then he found a loophole and a corrupt official. You see, in order to drill, ArBonCo had to pay the government for the rights because it's Curaçao land – that's what the contract was, a document giving them the right to drill. But Hearst inflated the price ArBonCo would pay – by fifty million dollars. ArBonCo would pay the government, then the official would use some very clever accounting to cream off the fifty million so the government only got what they expected, then the official would transfer twenty-five million dollars back to Hearst.'

Alex picked up his basket. 'Whereas now, they're taking early retirement in jail.'

'Only Hearst, I'm afraid,' said Bowman. 'There's not enough proof to implicate his accomplice. He was clever about covering his tracks.'

Amber's hand dropped from her chin. 'We know who he is,' she insisted. 'Simon Ter Haar.'

Bowman looked at her. 'I know who it is too, but we have no proof. Yet. It looks like Hearst did most of the running, even if Ter Haar did most of the thinking. Still, the fact that Hearst is in jail will be enough for me. His betrayal was by far the worst. And I have some very clever people looking at all the records to see if we can nail Ter Haar too. But at the moment, yes, he's still free.'

The others read the disappointment in Amber's face. The memory of the time she'd spent in Ter Haar's house wasn't going to go away in a hurry.

She swallowed hard. Bad flashbacks were one of the hazards of a job like this. You had to deal with them. She closed her eyes. After a while, the gentle rasp of trowel on wet sand and the voices of her friends made her feel more calm.

'What's going to happen to the tanker?' said Paulo.

'I'm having it removed by a specialist team,' said Bowman. 'No more accidents.'

'What about the concert?' said Li.

'It's rescheduled for next week. But I'm afraid if you come you'll have to hear me make my long boring speech about a prosperous future looking after the environment.'

Amber opened her eyes and looked out into the bay. She felt optimistic. And now that she looked, something *was* different. At first she couldn't see what had changed. Then she realized – the sorbent booms had gone. The horizon was clear, the sea was blue. It would be some time before the ecosystem recovered, but the view looked almost normal again.

Behind her, Lynn, Danny and Carl watched from the bar window. Lynn had taken a few pictures and was showing them to the two men, clicking them up on the display on the back of the camera.

'That'll make a nice story,' said Danny quietly.

'Yeah,' agreed Carl. He imagined the headline: BILL BOWMAN, BACK IN CHARGE AND SHOWING THE WAY AHEAD.

Lynn walked through to her office and sat down at the phone. But before she phoned Ray on the *Amigoe*, she had another call to make. She dialled her sister.

'Sarah? There's something I want you to do.'

EPILOGUE

Simon Ter Haar manoeuvred his Mercedes into the garage, put the handbrake on and cut the engine. The silence was welcome – peace and quiet at last. As he pulled the key out he let his forehead rest on the leather steering wheel for a moment.

It had been a draining day – the police coming into the department, questioning him, looking through the files. But they hadn't found anything. Thank goodness he'd been careful. There were only two links to Hearst. First there were the calls on his mobile, but he'd got that covered; he had bought a pay-as-you-go unit from a dodgy dealer on a back street in Willemstad for cash so no one could trace it, and when everything went wrong he'd taken the sim card out and dropped it down a drain. Now no one could tell they'd ever talked to one another. The second link was in the e-mails. Ter Haar was a bit more worried about these. He'd been very discreet – there was nothing specific – but how long would it be before the police started asking questions about them? He would have to play it very, very cool.

The hit man might have been a problem, but he'd got away. The police had followed him to a cavern by the coast and then he had, quite simply, disappeared. They had found his boat, abandoned, but nothing else, and had concluded that he must have had a cache of dive gear in the cave and escaped underwater. Ter Haar could well believe it. 'John', if that was his name, had always been self-sufficient and secretive from the word go. It was a relief not to have him in the house any more.

Ter Haar reached for his Gucci briefcase and got out of the car. He slammed the door hard. How frustrating for all that work to come to nothing.

Months of planning and hopes had gone down the drain with that sim card. Ter Haar blamed Hearst. He'd been outsmarted by a bunch of environmentalists who didn't even look old enough to be out of school. It was right that Hearst should end up in jail – for being stupid.

Ter Haar put his key in the front door. It's time to calm down, he told himself. And indeed, just seeing the fine grain of the antique oak made him feel better. Inside was his oasis, his beautiful things that made the world feel special.

He twisted the key and stepped into the tiled hall.

It was when he closed the door that he noticed the smell. Heavy, like sulphur. Perhaps the drains were leaking.

'Mary?' he called. He listened for his housekeeper's response. No one replied. She must be out in the laundry room. Or maybe it was her evening off. He'd speak to her about it tomorrow. He put his keys on the marble hall table and went through to the lounge.

The smell was so strong it nearly made him retch. And what was all this?

A black mess, frosted with sand, lay in the middle of his pale grey carpet. At first he couldn't work out what it was; just a spiky jumble of rubbish dug up from the beach. Then his brain began to make sense of it – a tumble of wings, beaks, claws and eyes.

Dead seabirds.

They lay in a heap like leaves collected for a bonfire. More had been dumped on the ivory sofa and chairs. Around each heap was a black halo, which the pale furnishings were soaking up like blotting paper.

There must have been hundreds of birds there, slowly bleeding seawater and oil.

His damask suite – grimy like a mechanic's overalls. His silk cushions – smeared like rags. His pure wool carpet. Stained like a garage floor.

He stepped back, gagging.

CHRIS RYAN'S TOP SAS TIPS FOR SAFETY AND SURVIVAL IN AND AROUND WATER

Water sports are a lot of fun but never forget that water is dangerous. If something goes wrong it takes only seconds to drown – and even if people are pulled out alive, they often die later in hospital. Here are my top ten tips for safety and survival in and around the water.

1. Learn to swim

Whether you're sailing, windsurfing, water skiing, kayaking, fishing, snorkelling or riding a jet ski the golden rule is – learn to swim. Even if you're on a boat and not intending to get wet, you might end up taking an unexpected dip! And the 'learn to swim' rule counts even if you're scuba diving. Just because you've got air tanks doesn't mean you're safe. If something goes wrong with your equipment, you need to know how to swim back to safety.

Ask your school about swimming lessons if you don't know how to swim, or find out where your local pool is.

2. Get proper training

Except in a dire emergency, Alpha Force would never try a new activity without getting tuition – and neither should you. If you want to go scuba diving, go on a proper course. You'll be shown all the kit and how to use it, as well as being able to practise vital skills like the hand signals Alpha Force use when diving. You'll also learn how to take off your regulator and mask underwater and put them back on. This is unbelievably scary the first few times because you're suddenly blind and unable to breathe – but you want to be prepared in case it happens to you for real when you're out.

Even simpler-looking sports like surfing have important safety rules. For instance, if you're surfing and you get a dunking, come up with your hands above your head. Your board will be whizzing around loose; if it hits you on the head it could knock you out or break your nose, whereas a whack on the arms probably won't hurt so much.

To be really safe, you could also learn lifesaving techniques – and of course brush up on first aid. Again, lifesaving lessons should be available through swimming clubs at your local pool.

3. Use the right kit

Boats should have lifejackets for everyone. Don't rely on recreational swimming aids such as lilos – they may look funkier but they are not tough enough to save you in a real emergency. Never water ski or get on a jet ski without a lifejacket; you can reach high speeds and if you fall off, you could be knocked unconscious and drown.

It's always colder on the water so when you're sailing take extra jumpers and waterproofs. The sun's stronger too; so don't forget SPF (sun protection factor) cream or you'll soon look like a lobster.

If you're surfing or diving in cold water always use a wetsuit. It's easy to get very cold underwater because water cools you down. If the temperature's really low you may need a drysuit instead, because you can wear thermals underneath. Don't underestimate the effect of cold; it can exhaust you quickly and put you in real danger.

Make sure equipment is well maintained. Surfboards may have sharp edges, broken fins, etc., which can injure you. Boats need to be serviced regularly, and make sure someone checks that you have enough fuel and battery power before you set out: you'll feel really silly if you run out! Boats should also have some kind of emergency signalling device – such as an *Emergency Position Radio Beacon (EPiRB)*. This sends out global marine distress signals to ships, planes and satellites. It should also be checked and everyone on the craft should know how to operate it. Everyone should also know where the life rafts are and how to operate them.

When you get back, do any essential maintenance on your equipment straight away: wash wetsuits and dive gear with fresh water and arrange for any necessary repairs. Don't just leave it all in a heap while you put your feet up for a nice refreshing drink, or you could forget to do it altogether!

4. Check the area first

Don't swim, sail or surf anywhere unless you know it's safe. On beaches there will be designated areas – stick to them. Even if the water outside these areas looks calm, there could be dangerous rocks or strong currents that can suck you under. Even the best swimmer can't fight a strong undercurrent so it's best to avoid them. There may also be certain times when the tides change and make watersports more hazardous.

Don't swim where others are sailing. In some conditions boats may not be able to see you.

Don't go out too deep. If the sea floor drops abruptly, not only will you be unable to put your feet down; it's also the most likely place to find strong currents.

Inland waters such as rivers and lakes can be just as dangerous as the open sea. Lakes can be very cold beneath the surface – so cold that you could go into shock if you fall in. The bottoms of lakes and rivers can be soft, uneven and changeable and there may be submerged objects that might damage your boat or injure you. River currents are often stronger than they appear (you can check by throwing in a twig).

If there are no signs or notices, don't assume the water is safe. Check with someone who knows the area – a shopkeeper, a caravan park owner or someone who lives nearby. They are likely to know the dangers.

When I was fifteen and just learning to dive, I learned the value of local knowledge. I was looking for lobsters in the North Sea with a mate, feeling my way through a bed of kelp more than two metres high. It was spooky and slimy and when I felt something pull me I thought it was kelp. But when I put my hand down to feel behind me, my fingers touched a head and a snout. Thoughts of terrifying creatures flashed through my mind and I surfaced in two seconds flat – only to find my mate had surfaced too and was bobbing in the water laughing at me. My hideous monster had been nothing more dangerous than a friendly seal. My mate had known they were there, but I hadn't – and I felt a right idiot.

5. Watch out for marine life

Shark-infested waters

Anywhere there is warm salt water, there are sharks. If you are out in the water and you spot a shark, obviously you have to get away. No, it's not cool to try to stroke it or ride it. Instead, stay calm and swim strongly and rhythmically back to land or your boat. If you thrash wildly on the surface, shrieking that there's a shark in the water, that's a sure way to get eaten.

The tiniest amount of blood in the water is like a dinner gong to a shark. So if you're in an area where sharks are known to visit and you cut yourself, get out straight away!

Don't swim or surf near people who are fishing – not only might you get caught up in their lines; their bait and the thrashing motion of the caught fish might attract sharks.

If you're spear fishing, don't tie your catch to yourself by a short line. A passing shark will think the fish is the garnish and you're the main course. Put your catch in a floating basket, or tie it to a line at least eight metres long. And make sure you have permission to fish – you could be killing endangered species, and a number of fish in warmer waters are poisonous to eat!

Other nasties in the sea

Although they may not try to eat you, many other creatures in warm coastal waters sting or bite. Some are poisonous, but even if they're not you might get a nasty wound. Mostly they are not aggressive – they attack when people do dumb things.

Never try to pat a sea creature, see what their skin feels like or feed them a titbit – you will definitely regret it.

In the shallows, watch what's under your feet. In some parts of the world, stingrays hide in the sand. It's easy to step on one – and their barbed tails are very painful and poisonous. Find out if there are stingrays in the area before you go in. Shuffle your feet rather than wade. Then, if a stingray is buried in the sand, your foot will nudge him and he'll take off to a quieter area before you stomp on him.

It's a good idea to wear some kind of foot protection anyway when in the water. Even if there aren't stingrays, there may be broken glass or sharp shells.

Another major hazard is jellyfish. They often drift ashore and die on the beach, where they look intriguing – particularly the blue Portuguese Man-of-War. Never touch them. Even though they're dead, they still sting. Yes, it may be tempting to pop the air bladder with your toe but don't – it's like stepping on a bed of hot coals.

When you're in the water, jellyfish are difficult to see, so look for signs on land. If a lot have been washed up on the shore, there are probably more of them alive in the water. And don't go in after a major storm – the waves break up the tentacles so that they can't be seen, but they can give you a painful sting.

If you're in the water with someone who gets stung by a jellyfish or a stingray, help them out as quickly as possible and get first aid.

6. Feet first

Don't dive into water unless you are absolutely sure of the depth and can see the bottom. Every year people are paralysed diving into shallow water in rivers and lakes. Always enter the water feet first.

7. Don't go alone

Even the best swimmers, sailors and surfers can get into trouble. If you're on your own there's no one to help or call for rescue, so don't be tempted to go out on the water without a companion.

Always let people know how long you'll be out. Tell someone where you are going, how long you will be there and when you expect to return. And stick to it; the emergency services will not be amused if they find that the reason you didn't come back was because you decided to take a snooze in your boat, or chat to fellow surfers.

8. Check the weather

Never swim or go out on a surfboard when the sea is rough or the waves are high – the current may drag you under. Wind on lakes can also cause choppy waves that make it dangerous to swim.

Get out of the water straight away if you see or hear a storm – water conducts electricity and you are far more likely to be struck by lightning.

Water sports enthusiasts take the weather very seriously. Be prepared to change your plans if the conditions look bad.

Never go out on the water after dark. You can't see depth or hazards. Night, dusk and dawn are the times when sharks are hunting. When you plan your trip, make sure you will be out of the water by dusk – so check and double-check that you've timed everything accurately.

9. Don't go if you don't feel 100 per cent well

To stay safe on – or in – water, you must be alert. You need to remember safe techniques and rules, and to have the discipline to react properly in an emergency. You can't do this if you're tired, have a sore throat or a cold.

Know your limits too – water sports are strenuous. If you're out and you start to feel tired or cold, head back. Don't try to keep up with a stronger, more skilled swimmer or encourage others to keep up with you.

Watch out for the *dangerous toos* – too tired, too cold, too far from safety, too much sun, too much strenuous activity.

Nil by mouth is a good rule to remember. Don't eat sweets or chew gum when out on the water – you could easily choke. Always wait for an hour after a meal before swimming – you may get cramp. This is incredibly painful and makes it very difficult to keep afloat.

10. Trouble

If you see someone in trouble

If you can rescue someone without going into the water yourself, take that option. They might be battling currents and hazards you can't see. Find a long item such as a broom handle and see if you can reach them with it, then tow them to safety. Never take personal risks to save someone – that will only mean two people have to be rescued.

If you get in trouble

Whether swimming or surfing, if you get in trouble signal for help. Shout – sound travels well over water. Wave with one arm (not both – you'll go under).

Don't panic: struggling will only exhaust you. And if you're being swept along by an undertow don't try to swim against it. Most people try to swim back towards the shore, but this will wear you out in no time. I made that mistake myself once. I was swimming off Palm Beach in Florida, USA, about fifty metres out. I turned round and tried to come back and suddenly found the beach was getting further away and the tide was carrying me out to sea! So instead I pointed myself at forty-five degrees to the beach so that I was using the current and not fighting it. It took a while to get back but at least I managed it!

If you're a long way from shore, give yourself rest breaks. The human body is less dense than seawater and if you just relax you will float. When you've caught your breath, swim on. If you have a surfboard with you, keep hold of it – it will help you relax and float.

If you are caught in a current on a river, float on

your back and travel downstream feet first. That way if you encounter any objects or debris, you hit them feet first – rather than headbutting them. Angle your travel so that you drift towards shore.

If you're on a boat that's in trouble, stay with it for as long as possible. Your best chance of survival is on a boat, even if it is disabled – not a life raft, which is easily punctured and difficult to steer. Only get in the life raft when you're up to your waist in water in your main boat.

BE SAFE!

Chris Ryan

Random House Children's Books and Chris Ryan would like to make it clear that these tips are aimed at helping to increase your knowledge of safety in this area, and to avoid accidents. We would recommend proper instruction and cannot accept any liability for inappropriate usage of these tips.

This isn't the first time Alpha Force have had to use their skills to survive in the sea. Their very first meeting was on board a ship sailing round the Indonesian islands. Turn over to find out more . . .

Extract from Alpha Force: Survival

Red Fox
0 009 43924 7

Somewhere in the Indonesian Archipelago . . .

It only takes an instant to die . . .

As he struggled to swim away from the huge wave that towered over him, Alex began to hear his father's voice in his head, patiently explaining the survival skills he had learned in the SAS. It was oddly comforting to listen to that calm, quiet voice and Alex found the strength to push himself on through the turbulent water, even though his muscles were almost useless with exhaustion.

It only takes an instant to die, continued his father's voice. *The way to survive is to make sure you never reach that instant. Are you listening, Alex? You need to understand how an accident happens. Most people think it explodes without warning – blam! Like a firework. But you look more closely at that accident and what do you see . . . ?*

'A fuse . . .' croaked Alex, forcing himself to take a few more strokes before floundering to a stop. 'There's always a fuse . . .'

He blinked the stinging seawater from his eyes and looked over his shoulder to see whether he was clear of the breaking wave. He groaned. All that effort and he had hardly moved. It was as though he had been treading water. The wave still towered over him, even higher now. It was a solid slab of black water, except at the top where there was a frayed edge of white foam. The wave had reached its crest and was beginning to curl over. In a few seconds, the whole weight of that wall of water would crash down on top of him.

Alex stopped swimming. He knew he was fighting a losing battle. Instead, he concentrated on breathing, topping up his system with as much oxygen as he could before the wave hit. He felt himself being tugged backwards as the surrounding water was sucked into the base of the breaking wave. Forcing his burning lungs to take in one more deep breath, he turned and dived down under the surface a second before the breaker crashed down on top of him.

Even under the water, Alex was overwhelmed by the impact. The breaker slammed him down and knocked all the air out of him with a casual efficiency that reminded him of his mother kneading dough. As he tumbled lazily through the water, drifting on the edge of consciousness, Alex thought about his mother making bread half a world away in the kitchen he had been so keen to leave. He thought of how sad she would be if he did not return from this trip and suddenly he was fully awake again.

He began to struggle against the current, which was still rolling him over and over, pulling him nearer and nearer to the reef where the boat had broken in two. If he was dragged across the razor-sharp coral, his skin would be torn to ribbons. How close was he? There was a roaring in his ears which could be breaking surf. Alex forced his eyes open, but it was so dark under the water, he could not tell which way was up. He redoubled his efforts to swim against the current until he felt as though his chest was about to burst open. His movements became weaker, the roaring in his ears grew louder and sparks of multi-coloured light began to dance behind his eyes, but he kept going and, suddenly, the current let him go. He broke surface and pulled whooping breaths of air into his lungs.

Clearing his eyes, he peered about him. The moon was up and, in its pale light, he could just see the dark, jagged outline of the island he was trying to reach. He turned in the water and saw white surf breaking on the reef behind him. It was still too close for comfort and another huge wave was beginning to build. Gritting his teeth, Alex started to swim again, scanning the water for any sign of the rest of A-Watch.

He spotted Amber first, way ahead of him. She had nearly reached the island and was swimming strongly. Behind Amber, but still in the quieter waters of the lagoon, two more heads bobbed close together in the water. Paulo and Li, thought Alex, guessing that Paulo would not leave Li's side if he could help it. But where was Hex? Alex felt a chill run through him as he remembered that Hex, the fifth member of A-Watch, had been even nearer to the reef before the wave hit.

Despite the next breaker building behind him, Alex slowed and turned to scan the surface for Hex. He half-expected to see a body, floating face down in a spreading circle of blood, but there was nothing. Then he caught a movement over to his left. There was Hex, ahead of him now, and swimming steadily towards the island. He must have managed to surf in on the back of the wave that had swallowed Alex.

Satisfied, Alex put the others out of his mind and concentrated on swimming as hard as he could. This time he was nearly clear of the breaker when it crashed. Once more, he dived to survive the impact, then swam against the current that was pulling him backwards. He felt a surge of elation as he broke surface again. He was going to make it! Then something slammed into the back of his head with bone-shattering force. Instinctively, he flung his left arm up to protect his head and was caught in a grip which instantly tightened, biting into the flesh of his wrist. As he began to spiral down into the water, trailing blood, Alex heard his father's voice again.

Every accident has a fuse, son. There's always a fuse.

Alex watched with a sort of dazed curiosity as a thin rope of his own blood twisted away from him towards the surface. That must be the fuse, he thought. In the few seconds left to him before he lost consciousness, Alex imagined the fuse stretching across the sea and back in time to twenty-four hours earlier, when they had all still been aboard the *Phoenix*. That was when it had all started. That final Watch Duty, when the fuse was lit . . .

About the Author

CHRIS RYAN joined the SAS in 1984 and has been involved in numerous operations with the Regiment. During the first Gulf War he was the only member of an eight-man team to escape from Iraq, three colleagues being killed and four captured. It was the longest escape and evasion in the history of the SAS. For this he was awarded the Military Medal. He wrote about his remarkable escape in the adult bestseller *The One Who Got Away* (1995), which was also adapted for screen.

He left the SAS in 1994 and is now the author of many bestselling thrillers for adults, as well as the *Alpha Force* series for younger readers. His work in security takes him around the world and he has also appeared in a number of television series, including *Hunting Chris Ryan*, in which his escape and evasion skills were demonstrated to the max, and *Pushed to the Limit*, in which Chris put ordinary British families through a series of challenges. On Sky TV he also appeared in *Terror Alert*, demonstrating his skills in a range of different scenarios.

CHRIS RYAN'S ALPHA FORCE - THE MISSIONS

Have you read them all . . . ?

SURVIVAL

The five members of Alpha Force meet for the first time when they survive a shipwreck and are marooned on a desert island.

RAT-CATCHER

Alpha Force fight to catch an evil drugs baron in South America.

DESERT PURSUIT

Alpha Force come face-to-face with a gang of child-slavers operating in the Sahara Desert.

HOSTAGE

When they are alerted to reports of illegal dumping of toxic waste, Alpha Force fly to Canada to investigate.

RED CENTRE

An Australian bushfire and a hunted terrorist test Alpha Force's skills to the limit.

HUNTED

Alpha Force find themselves in a desperate battle with a ruthless band of ivory poachers in Zambia.

BLOOD MONEY

While they are in southern India, Alpha Force learn of a growing trade in organ transplants from living donors and must locate a young girl before it's too late.

FAULT LINE

Disaster strikes when a massive earthquake devastates a built-up area in Belize.

BLACK GOLD

Alpha Force are diving in the Caribbean when an oil tanker runs aground and when an assassin strikes they need all their skills to survive.

UNTOUCHABLE

Alpha Force must unearth the truth about the mysterious activity on a laird's estate in the Scottish Highlands.